Bolton
Council

23. 04. 09.

21. NOV 10.

Jason Kilkenny's Gun

Josh Kincaid was young; too young to be skipping school and day-dreaming about the outlaws and gunfighters he read about in the dime novels he hid from his parents and his town marshal uncle. Then, when he found injured bounty hunter Rance Savage and brought him into town, Josh found himself under the spell of a real life hero.

But Savage was obsessed by an old grudge; filled with a bitter rancour against the man who had crippled him and left him to die. Nothing but full retribution would quell the bitterness he carried within him. Like the LeMat revolver he wore, the man was cold and deadly, an instrument of revenge.

Before he realized what was happening, Josh would become the mankiller's unwitting accomplice in a scheme of vengeance that would tear the town apart and shatter his family.

Jason Kilkenny's Gun

Kit Prate

A Black Horse Western

ROBERT HALE · LONDON

© Kit Prate 2008
First published in Great Britain 2008

ISBN 978-0-7090-8678-9

Robert Hale Limited
Clerkenwell House
Clerkenwell Green
London EC1R 0HT

www.halebooks.com

The right of Kit Prate to be identified as
author of this work has been asserted by her
in accordance with the Copyright, Designs and
Patents Act 1988

*For Justin, My Own One in One Thousand; and for Dave
Matijevich, Compadre.*

PROLOGUE

Growing up is painful. It's not just the stabbing night pains that gnaw at the long muscles in the back of a young boy's legs, nor is it the pleasant hurt that comes with the sudden rush of awakening manhood when that boy steals his first real kiss. It is the inner pain, the tight chest that surrounds a heart grown large with great fear and even greater despair, and the throbbing eyes that are suddenly dry because the passage of a certain number of years declares the boy a man. A man who can no longer show a boy's grief, or weep a boy's tears. These are the real pains of growing up.

Joshua Kincaid grew up the spring of '98, the same spring he turned sixteen.

The same spring he found Jason Kilkenny's gun.

CHAPTER 1 ^{PB}

Kincaid woke slowly, grimacing at the Charley horse in his right shoulder. He eased his arm from beneath his wife's head, slowly, taking great pains not to waken her. Shaking his numb fingers, he flexed the arm, working the soreness out of the tight muscles and tender joints.

It had been a long night, unusually warm for spring, and the baby had fussed and fretted into the pink hours just before dawn. She was cutting teeth, slowly, one small nub at a time.

The man inhaled, lying back against the pillow, his hands locked behind his head. He was getting too old for this kind of misery. *Two hours*, he mused, reaching out to the small table beside the bed for his pocket watch. The knowledge brought a series of long yawns. Two hours of sleep, and a full day ahead of him. Resigned, he sat up, cursing as the bedsprings squalled beneath him. He cast a fleet look at the quiet form of his wife, relieved that she still slept. *I'm getting too old for this proud papa thing, Sarah*, he scolded mentally.

Reaching out, he smoothed the long hair away from the woman's eyes. Too old. His fingers lingered on her cheeks. She brushed at his fingers with the back of her hand, still asleep, moving as she would to shoo away a marauding mosquito. Kincaid studied her face, the flawless profile. A petulant frown tugged briefly at the corner of her mouth, the lines smoothing. She looked more little girl than grown

7

woman, snuggling into the man's touch.

The woman had turned on her back, her breasts firm and full beneath the white flannel gown. She raised one arm over her head, and a wet spot formed against the soft fabric, the moist cloth becoming translucent over the peaked breast. Kincaid's hand trailed down the woman's cheek . . . her neck . . . closing gently to cup the woman's fullness in his palm. He grinned, feeling a flood of warmth washing through his belly. *Too old to play papa*, he thought, pleased with himself, *but sure in hell not too old for all the things that went beforehand.* He leaned over, his lips warm and soft on the woman's throat. He wouldn't wake her – couldn't, knowing her fatigue – but come noon, when the baby was down for a nap, and the house was empty. . . .

The harsh sound of metal clanging against metal roused the man from his reverie, and he sat back up, scratching himself. He pivoted off the bed and stood, crossing the floor to the chair where he had hung his pants.

He was a lean man, a week past forty-two, his tanned face setting off a pair of startling, pale-blue eyes that dominated the high cheekbones and well-defined chin. A carefully trimmed mustache cut a precise path across his upper lip, matching the full head of dark hair he had inherited from his mother. There were laugh lines at the corners of his eyes, deep, and they softened the strong face and made it gentle.

Still conscious of the sleeping woman, Kincaid slipped into his trousers. The chambray work shirt was next, and he sucked in his flat belly as he tucked the tail into the top of his summer longjohns. There was a dull ache in his groin. In his mind, he knew that he would have to wait to be alone with the woman, but the rest of his body. . . . He shook his head, cursing the tightness at his crotch as he buttoned his pants.

The baby whimpered, and Kincaid tiptoed quickly to the small trundle bed. He never tired of looking at her. She was the image of Sarah. A surprise, to be sure – God only knows, she wasn't planned – and in a way, a miracle. A second chance, he thought soberly. He reached out, his forefinger slipping through the silky softness of the child's blonde curls. An honest-to-God second chance.

The noises from the kitchen came again, filtering through the closed door, and Kincaid adjusted the blanket around the infant's shoulders. He took one last look at both mother and child, and then picked up his boots.

Jake was at the stove, coaxing a fire under the enamel coffee pot. He slid the grate back in place, wincing as the grid slipped and clattered shut. The noise tore at him and he cursed softly. 'Shit!'

Kincaid eyed his brother, leaning against the wall as he tugged at his boots. He stamped his feet, lightly, tamping the mule-ears in place. 'Long night, Jake?' he whispered.

'No,' the other snapped, his tone caustic. 'Ain't nothin' I like more than playin' daddy to a county jail road crew while our duly appointed sheriff sits on his fat ass at the capital. . . .'

J.T. raised his hands, calling a halt to the tirade. He crossed the floor to the shelves above the sink, taking down two cups, and returned to the stove. 'You could have told Lathrop *no*, Jake.' He held out both cups.

Jake did the honors, filling both mugs. He topped off his own with a healthy shot from the small flask he carried in his hip pocket. 'I needed the money,' he said, avoiding his brother's scrutiny. 'I always pay for my own extras, J.T., and there's a lot more to my life than one woman' – he nodded toward the hallway – 'and a bunch of sassy kids.' The grin softened the man's harsh declarations.

J.T. shook his head, blowing into his cup. 'There doesn't have to be,' he chided, sensing the emptiness. 'The ranch is doing well enough to support two families, Jake, if we're careful. And Clara Altman—'

Jake cut his brother short with a curt wave of his hand '— won't have me unless I give up this,' he tapped the silver star with his index finger. He shrugged, pretending it didn't matter. *That Clara Altman didn't matter.*

'Then do it,' J.T. advised, his tone as abrupt as his words. 'Give it up and start ranching full time.'

Jake exhaled slowly. It was an old argument, and he knew that J.T.'s patience was wearing thin. He finished his coffee, feeling his brother's eyes on him, *on the pistol he wore at his right hip.* Without thinking, he fingered the walnut grip. 'I can't,' he breathed. He swung his head around, facing the other's hard stare. Excepting for the difference in eye coloring – Jake's eyes were a cold chestnut brown – it was like looking in a mirror. 'I'm no good at ranching, J.T.; never have been.' He stroked the butt of his revolver. '*This* is all I'm good at, all that I've ever been good at.'

J.T. put his cup down on the table, hard. 'You're wrong, Jake,' he said stubbornly. 'It's just that *that*' – he paused, gesturing at the man's hip – 'is the only thing you've ever really worked at.'

Jake shook his head, weary. 'No more sermons, *hermano*,' he sighed. 'I am what I am, and it's too late to change any of it.' He felt a need to change the subject, and combed his fingers through his dark hair. 'The heifer's gone,' he said finally. 'I saw the poles down when I rode in. She must have busted out last night after everyone went to bed. . . .'

J.T. swore under his breath. He stared down the hallway leading to the back bedrooms. Josh, he thought darkly. The boy was always daydreaming, rushing through his chores. Careless. Kincaid shook his head. *So much for your all-day fishing trip, son,* he lamented. *And whatever else you had figured for your Saturday romp.* Resolute, he headed for the boy's bedroom.

The old he-wolf moved to the mouth of the cave, his nose lifted to a new scent brought by the shifting north winds. He moved slowly, with great effort, his hind legs stiff from the damp *caliche* and early morning cold. The massive head

10

lifted higher, the black nostrils moist, dilating as he tested the air. His left ear came forward sharply, the tattered right ear limp, its cartilage mutilated and softened in one too many battles. The amber eyes stared beyond the yellow-white rock outcroppings, the hair on the animal's back coming forward, then smoothing as the wind changed and the air became clean and sweet once more. Raising his nose to the cold blue sky, the animal began to howl. The tormented wail ended suddenly, the noise of a rifle exploding into the wilderness quiet.

Rance Savage felt no remorse as the gray wolf fell. He pulled the Henry away from his cheek, staring down the side of the hill. He was tired and in need of a warm place to spend the coming day; someplace where he could have a fire to ease the congestive ache in his chest, and the older pain in his stiff left knee. Someplace where he could sit without his back to the wall, and – if he was lucky – steal a few hours of much needed sleep. He pushed the rifle back over his shoulder, adjusting the strap so that the weapon rested comfortably between his shoulder blades, and limped back to his horse.

He was on the run; had been, ever since he made the mistake of killing a sheriff during an argument over the lawman's demand for a share of the bounty money. And now he needed some miles between himself and the Texas law; miles and time. Lots of time.

The contest with the El Paso constable had been even-handed. At least Savage considered it to have been fair. He had given the man plenty of warning; repeated warnings. But it hadn't mattered. Not to the town, and not to the lawman's family. Savage cursed his bad luck, drawing his long coat up around his neck.

It spooked him, this feeling of being hunted. For years, he had been the pursuer, the hunter. *It's wrong,* he thought bitterly. *I don't give a damn what the Texas law thinks.* He swore, cursing them all.

11

The limp was worse as he led the long-limbed Tennessee walking horse down the rock-strewn trail to his temporary sanctuary. The dark gelding balked, his head coming up as they approached the wolf's carcass. Savage swore again and jerked hard on the horse's bridle. *Damned thorobred.* The animal was a running fool when he moved, but nervous and high strung; spooked silly by any sudden movement – the rustle of a cigarette paper, the rattle of the dry pods in the tall catalpa trees. Silently, Savage made himself a promise. First chance he found another animal, the gelding was going.

They entered the cavern, the horse hanging back a second time, his front legs rigid as he searched the dark hole with white-ringed eyes. Savage used the quirt this time, and the animal responded in kind. The horse bared its teeth, raking across the sleeve of Savage's heavy coat, a slimy string of saliva leaving a long trail against the matted buffalo wool. And then, submissive, the gelding followed the man inside, and, just as submissively, accepted the leather hobbles.

Savage built a small fire, raking up the litter from the cavern floor. He fanned the red, burning twigs, coaxing a bigger flame. The fire rose toward the low ceiling, the smoke spiraling upwards toward some unseen air shaft, the orange light drawing exaggerated shadows on the smudge-streaked walls.

The cave had been used before, the marks of old fires faded a smoky gray against the pink and yellow sandstone. Savage stood up, rubbing his hands above the flame, his eyes exploring the hole. It was larger than he first suspected, a dome-shaped room with the floor space of a small cabin. 'Or a cell,' he said aloud. The laughter that rolled from between his lips was devoid of any humor.

Savage set about preparing his supper. He couldn't remember the last time he had enjoyed the luxury of a hot meal. He smiled the grim smile a second time. Cold beans, dried beef and canned milk had been his bill of fare for three long months. The memory of the cold suppers made the side meat smell that much sweeter.

Savage hunkered down on the floor of the cave, his stiff left leg extended, and pried open a second can of beans. These he poured on top of the salted pork. Taking a large spoon from his mess kit, he stirred the last of his brown sugar into the pot, and watched as the mixture began to simmer above the flames.

Impatient, the man scooped up a generous spoonful of beans, filling his mouth. The hot beans stuck in his throat when he attempted to swallow, and he gagged at the fire tearing at his Adam's apple. The food lodged halfway and seemed to hang there. The coughing began, the deep, wet hacking that had plagued him for more weeks than he could remember, his shoulders heaving as the great spasms tore at his chest. There was no release for the thick phlegm that now crowded his choked airway, and he felt the panic of a drowning man.

He stood up, gasping desperately for air, the pot clanging on to the littered floor. His face a deep purple, Savage groped his way toward the sunlight at the face of the cave, an ache deep in his chest as the coughing continued. He made it as far as the remains of the dead wolf, and then collapsed. He fell face forward, striking his head on the rock-littered clay and landing on his belly. The food that was lodged in his windpipe spewed from his mouth as he sank into a dark oblivion.

'Dammit, Will, let's go home.' Josh Kincaid stretched, trying to ease the sore muscles in his lower back, his eyes on his older brother.

Will shook his head without turning around. 'Pa sent us out here to find that heifer calf, and we're going to find her.'

Josh swore. 'To hell with that goddamn calf!' He touched his heels to the sides of his sorrel mare, and moved to catch

13

up with his brother.

Will kept staring straight ahead, his lips a tight line. At nineteen – a shorter version of his father and his uncle – he was more focused on the job at hand than his towheaded sibling. It was not just the four years that separated him from Josh, there was a difference in temperament as well. Will was serious, hardworking and dependable. He never started a job he didn't see through to the finish. He spoke, eventually, his voice filled with even more censure than his words. 'We wouldn't be out here, Josh, if you had fixed the fence proper in the first place.'

Josh's face flared red. He was still smarting from the reprimand his pa had given him. 'I did fix it!' he snapped, his voice rising. It was a poor lie. He should have reset the corner poles, strung more new wire and been more careful when he spliced the old. 'I did fix it,' he repeated softly, under his breath.

Will just shook his head; he was all too familiar with Josh's excuses and lame explanations. He pulled up, putting his hand out to grab Josh's knee. 'Up there, Josh. Just above the creek.' He nodded in the direction of the water. Josh followed his brother's gaze, his eyes smarting from the sun. He had forgotten his hat again. Squinting, he shaded his eyes with his right hand.

The heifer lay beside the shallow stream, her head backward over one shoulder. There was a dark, red-brown smear at her throat, and the iridescent blue green of swarming flies.

Will was quiet again, his changing posture indicating his current mood. He clucked softly to his dun gelding, urging the animal into the water. Josh followed, knowing what they would find, wishing that his brother would say something, anything. He hated the silent, unspoken disapproval that hung between them. It would be a long ride back to the ranch.

Both boys dismounted, Will going directly to the spotted she-calf. He dropped down on one knee, his eyes studying the moist ground around the heifer's torn front quarters. 'Old Three-Toes,' he whispered, fingering the deep imprint in the wet sand. His hand moved gently down the dead calf's side, as if she were alive and he was petting her. He held out his hand, his fingers wiggling. 'I need your knife.' If he did things right, he could at least salvage a portion of the hide.

Josh felt a sinking deep down in his chest. 'I haven't got it,' he said softly.

'What?' Will looked up at his younger brother, his eyebrows coming together in a deep frown.

Josh gritted his teeth. The knife had been new; it hadn't been a week since he'd talked his pa into buying it. 'I lost it.' He didn't give a damn anymore what Will might think, the anger in his words. 'I don't know where, Will,' he yelled, anticipating the question. 'And I don't know when! I just know it's gone!'

Will's shoulders drooped momentarily, and then he dug into his own pocket. He pulled out a single-bladed knife and began sawing away at the heifer's hide. The small blade punctured the skin on the animal's exposed hind leg, and the boy began skinning. It was tedious work, the boy's forehead and neck beginning to redden and fleck with sweat. He went about the grim, laborious task silently, uncomplaining.

Josh took Will's continued silence as one more rebuke. He hated the way his older brother could make him feel; like he still wore three-cornered pants and couldn't stay dry. The youngster kicked at a rock, watching as it plunked into the water. There wasn't much about Will that he didn't hate – leastwise, that's how it seemed. Will never did anything wrong. He always had his chores done, was on time for meals, and kept his side of the room straight. *Will*, he thought bitterly, *could put on his Sunday suit, fall down in a pile of fresh cowshit, and get up looking and smelling like he'd just taken a bath.*

Josh, on the other hand, always seemed to be in trouble. Like with the heifer. He forced himself to look at the calf.

They had put her in a separate pen, weaning her away from the family milk cow, and it had been his job to see that she stayed penned. But all the animal did was stand butting her head against the poles until she knocked them loose and the wire sagged, and then she'd be gone. And he would be in trouble again.

The boy's eyes drifted away from the dead animal, exploring the wet ground around the carcass. The wolf tracks were large, the print of the right forepaw minus one digit. Josh knelt down in the damp sand, spreading his hand over the deep impression. Will was right. It was Three-Toes. His face brightened, and he stood up. He helped himself to the small-bore rifle from this brother's saddle scabbard. 'I'm going to shoot me a wolf, Will,' he said, backing away. He didn't wait for any response, just hop-scotched across the stream on a pathway of exposed, moss-covered rock.

'Josh!!' Will looked up from his work, his eyes on his brother's back. 'Josh!!'

The fleeing boy grinned, pretending not to hear, and sprinted up into the foothills. He knew where he was going. He had known about the cave for a long time; had trailed the ancient wolf one long winter afternoon when he was supposed to have been at school. He envied the animal's freedom, his reputation among the small ranchers that populated the valley. Old Three-Toes was a legend. Werewolf, the old men called him. A shape-shifter that came with the night and descended on the valley, only to disappear with the morning mists. Josh had laughed at their stories. The old wolf was real. He knew that as well as he knew his own name.

He had seen the animal; had seen and tracked him. Had stood in the rocks above the Sweetwater to watch as the crafty man-wise deceiver backtracked and led a neighboring rancher and his hired hands on a wild goose chase.

The sun was hot on the boy's neck as he clambered up the side of the sandstone arroya toward the rock outcroppings that hid the entrance to the cave. He paused, checking the rifle. Killing the old wolf was not a thing he longed to do, but it would mean a respite from his pa's disappointment and anger over the slaughtered calf. And he knew he would be able to get downwind, close enough for a killing shot, even with the .22. The old wolf was almost deaf, and his eyesight was failing. Yet, even with his infirmities, the animal had retained his freedom.

But only because of the cave.

The sandstone escarpment was in two tiers, the uppermost extending two feet out and above the lower, with both a front and back entrance. Josh dug into the old familiar handholds, straining to reach up with one hand to deposit the rifle on the rock shelf above him. He hung there, suspended high above the winding creek bed, and then, using both arms, he pulled himself up on to the flat rock.

He rested on his belly for a time, his head buried in his arms as his breathing returned to normal. Then, slowly, he lifted his head, his right hand reaching for the rifle.

The entrance to the cavern was plainly visible. There was something on the ground in front of the black hole. Dark, furry, like a small bear, yet somehow different. Whatever it was, it was sprawled across the corpse of the old wolf.

Josh rose up on one elbow. He was a good hundred yards from the wolf's den, and he lay quietly, debating his next move. In his mind's eye, he drew fantasies of what must have happened, the way the old wolf must have died. The animal would have fought to his death to defend his secret place, and would have taken his attacker with him. Using the rifle as a staff, the boy rose up on his knees and pulled himself erect. There was a sadness in him as he approached the creatures sprawled on the ground.

He reached the pair, realizing for the first time that the thing he had thought an animal was a man in a buffalo hide coat. A big man, six feet or more in height, with immense, well-muscled shoulders and long-fingered hands. Laying the rifle aside, Josh reached out, his fingers probing at the long artery in the man's neck. Suddenly, a hand closed around his lower arm, a vise squeezing against the fragile bones in his wrist.

And then the voice came, weak, barely above a whisper. 'I need help, boy.' The fingers tightened, and the man repeated the words, louder. '*I need help.*'

CHAPTER 2

'Doc's,' Will said finally. 'I'll have to take him to Doc Harper's.' The young man frowned, his fingers tracing the scars on the big gelding's dark flank. 'I don't think much of a man that would mark a horse like this,' he complained. His eyes worked carefully over the man's gear. A short-barreled shotgun was strapped in easy reach behind the cantle; an army issue Henry in the saddle scabbard. Beneath the bulge in the man's heavy coat there was an open-tipped holster. A LeMat pistol fitted snugly in the leather sheath, the holster on a swivel, the tanned hide cut away to expose the trigger.

'You take my horse, Josh. Tell Pa what we found, and where I am.' He took a step toward his brother's mare.

'No!' Josh blocked his brother's way. He vaulted up into the saddle. 'You tell Pa!' Angry, he nodded at the now unconscious form tied upright on the other horse. His chin jutted out. '*I'm* taking him to town, Will.' There was a belligerence in the boy's tone. 'I found him, and *I'm taking him in*!' Backing away from his brother, he took a proprietary hold on the man's horse.

Will studied his brother's face. There were times when he desperately wished his pa wasn't so disinclined to physical punishment, and this was one of them. More and more, with each passing day, Josh was getting out of hand. He didn't listen to anyone anymore. 'All right,' he said finally. 'You take him into Doc's, Josh.' He reached up, his hand closing on

19

Josh's right leg. 'And then you fetch Uncle Jake, and come home.' He saw the sudden refusal in his brother's eyes, and tightened his grip. 'I mean it, Josh. You take him to Doc's, you get Uncle Jake, and then you come home!'

The younger boy started to shake his head, and then reconsidered as he felt his brother's fingers digging into his knee. There was only so far he could push Will, and he knew that he had reached that point. 'All right! I'll do it all, just like you want! Take him to Doc's, fetch Uncle Jake, and come home,' he mimicked. There was a mocking in his tone, a sing-song whine, as he repeated the list of instructions. 'You satisfied?' He wrenched free of Will's grasp and kicked the mare in the sides, taking his anger at his brother out on the animal. Swearing, he tugged the dark gelding's reins, jerking harder when the stranger's big horse balked.

Josh took the rim trail into Sonoita, moving at a slow walk, looking back again and again at the hunched-over man. He seemed more dead than alive, rocking limply back and forth, held in place more by sheer iron will than the ropes. It was a long ride, five miles of saw-tooth grades that punished both horse and rider. For a time, Josh envied his silent companion's dulled state, rubbing at the cramping pains in his own young legs.

Gradually, the road leveled off, and the schoolhouse slowly appeared on the dim horizon. The tilted weather-vane on the top of the bell tower, then the gray shingled roof, and finally, the faded clapboard siding. It was the first time Josh had ever welcomed the sight of the oppressively confining building.

He nudged the sweating sorrel into a slow trot as the road smoothed, and cut between the school and the privy to the main street. He could feel the eyes of the townspeople on him, hear their whispers, and pulled himself straight with an air of new-found importance. Terse, he waved aside their questions, moving through the milling collection of men that had gathered beside him. He led the tall gelding straight toward the rambling brick building that served as combination mortuary and doctor's office.

Willing hands reached out to help him, and together he and two of the men from Fulton's Saloon pulled the big man from the black horse. Josh could smell the sour odor of whiskey on their breath, conscious of their labored breathing as they struggled with their burden.

Harper was at the door of his office. He was a long, gaunt man whose once boyish face was already showing the signs of premature age. He led the way to the examining table, helping to position the man beneath the two hanging lanterns. Businesslike, he waved the curious bystanders away, his questions directed at Josh. 'Where'd you find him, son?' he asked, struggling with the bone fasteners on the heavy coat.

'Up on the Sweet,' Josh answered, purposely vague. No one knew about the cave; not Will, not anyone. It was his secret place, and he had no desire to share it.

The doctor nodded, satisfied. He pulled the coat away from the injured man's chest, raising his hand and signaling for quiet. Intent, he pressed his ear to the man's left side, his brow furrowing as he concentrated on the sounds. He raised up, measuring the man's bulk with a practiced eye. Two hundred pounds easy, he reckoned, noting the man's massive shoulders. 'How the hell did you get him on his horse?' he asked, his fingers probing at the carotid artery. He was nodding his head slowly, in time with the weak pulse that beat beneath his fingertips.

'He climbed aboard himself, Doc. Then he passed out, and I tied him.' Josh moved closer to the table, his eyes locked on the holster at the man's waist. Covetously, he reached out, fingering the LeMat's ivory grip.

There was the soft shuffle of booted feet as the men in the doorway stepped aside. It was obvious from the heavy, precise footfall that Jake Kincaid had entered the building. He crossed the room to the table, facing Josh, and reached out,

21

turning the injured man's face to the light. His set lips turned downward suddenly, and he shoved the man's head away, wiping his palm on his vest as if he had touched something unclean. 'How bad, Doc?'

Harper had seen the lawman's move. Even more, he had seen the look on the marshal's face. 'He's got pneumonia,' he breathed, 'maybe worse.' He tapped the man's chest, shaking his head.

'He going to die?' The question came suddenly, no real concern or compassion in Kincaid's voice. He dug into his pocket for his tobacco, slowly building a smoke, ignoring the doctor's disapproving frown.

'I don't know,' Harper answered evenly. 'Depends on how he responds to treatment.'

Kincaid nodded his head, his dark eyes cold. He moistened the edge of the fragile paper with his tongue and joined the edges, twisting one end between his thumb and forefinger. 'Let him die,' he ordered.

The room filled with a series of frenzied murmurs, and the sound grew in intensity until Kincaid silenced it with an abrupt wave of his hand. 'He's a bounty hunter,' he said scornfully. 'Rance Savage.' The whispers rose again, and his eyes narrowed as he paused to strike a match against a nail on the heel of Savage's boot. 'Fifteen hundred, or fifteen dollars, it never made a damn to Rance.' The lawman laughed, but there was no humor in the sound. 'He'd kill his own brother for a dime; buy a nickel cartridge, and kill for the nickel profit.'

Harper was still busy working on Savage. 'I'm a physician, Jake, not a judge or jury.' He stared across at the lawman, his voice hard, quiet. 'You have any paper on him?'

Kincaid's jaws tightened. He'd known Harper a long time. The man had principles; something, under these circumstances, that the lawman considered a great flaw. 'No,' he replied, his tone matching the doctor's. 'No papers.'

'Fine,' Harper grunted. He turned back to his patient, dismissing the lawman as just one more intruder. No one moved; not the crowd, not the lawman. His hands still busy, Harper lifted his eyes to the room full of people, probing the faces one by one. He exchanged a long, final look with Kincaid. 'Get out of my office, Jake,' he ordered. 'And take the rest of these' – he struggled for the right word –'gentlemen with you.'

Josh exhaled sharply at the physician's words, his mouth dropping open. No one talked to Jake like that, not ever! The crowd seemed to diminish, backing away from the two men. They stood there, staring hard at each other, Savage on the table between them like some great barricade; the doctor on one side, the lawman on the other.

Kincaid was the first to yield. He swung his eyes from the physician to the crowd of men, sweeping them from the room *en masse* with a silent, baleful glare.

The dark look shoved Josh farther back into the shadowed corner where he stood apart from the others. The boy averted his eyes when his uncle turned to face him. He remained rooted to the place where he stood, pretending not to see the single finger the man waggled at him. Kincaid bristled visibly at his nephew's stubborn pretense, his back rigid. He stood for a time, silent, expectant. And then, disgusted, he turned on his heel and followed the retreating crowd into the street.

Josh watched as Harper worked. The big man on the table fascinated him, and he could not stop himself from gawking. He inched forward, mindful of the doctor's mood, exploring the injured man with his eyes.

Harper had, with considerable difficulty, removed the heavy hair coat. The bounty hunter lay flat and silent on the narrow table, his boots extending a good three inches over the edge. He was as massive, as formidable as he had seemed when covered by the great coat. There was not one shred of soft flesh on him, and his shoulders . . . Josh took a step closer.

The man had the biggest set of shoulders the boy had ever seen. Thick, well-fleshed, the muscles at his neck extending in a smooth, tight line down across the collar bone, bulging prominently at his shoulders and upper arms. *Like a bear*, Josh thought. *As awesome and as terrible as a great bull bear.*

Savage. The name seemed to fit. Josh probed his memory, trying to remember where he had heard the name. An excitement touched him then, and he moved to the side of the table for a closer look at the man's face. There wasn't a schoolboy in the Territory that didn't know the name, the legends. In the boy's mind, Savage became one with Old Three-Toes. A rebel. An outlaw loner who shunned the pack and thumbed his nose at the rules. He closed his eyes tight, and silently willed the man to live.

'Josh?'

Will Kincaid stood in the narrow doorway, a frown pulling at the corners of his mouth. His eyes swept across the still form on the doctor's table, finally settling on the equally quiet form of his younger brother. 'Pa says you're to come home, Josh.' He paused, cocking his head when he saw the refusal filling the boy's eyes. 'Now, Josh,' he said quietly.

The younger boy hesitated. He was measuring Will with his eyes, his mind. He shook his head, filled with an anger he had to push into the pit of his stomach. *For now.* But someday, he promised himself, *someday. . . .* Will called to him again and, unwillingly, Josh followed him out into the street.

The family was at the table, finishing the last of their early Monday morning breakfast. Josh was cramming the food into his mouth, eating and talking at the same time. 'He's huge, Ma!' He gestured with his arms outstretched, as if he were telling a great fish story. 'And the guns, Ma. . . .'

Sarah Kincaid reached out, pressing her fingers against the boy's lips. She shook her head when he started to protest. 'You're going to be late for school, Josh.' She nodded toward the stack of books on the dry sink, and held out her other hand, the boy's lunch pail dangling from her fingers.

Crestfallen, the boy took the tin. Nobody ever listened to him. They all sat here, around the same little table, content to live their lives as though there was nothing else, no other way to live; no world beyond this small place. He shook his head at their lack of understanding, his eyes meeting his father's.

J.T. smiled across the rim of his coffee cup, blowing into the steaming mug. He winked at his son. 'He's a man, Josh. Just an ordinary man,' he chided gently.

Josh felt his face flush a bright red. He had thought that his pa, at least, would understand. His pa was interested in everything, just like he was. They shared a common love for so many things: for the land, for the things that moved on top and beneath it. Even Old Three-Toes. Josh thought of the many times he'd heard his father's quiet wish that the old wolf would run free, free from the men that were always pursuing him. 'Pa. . . .'

J.T. reached out, his fingers closing around the boy's arm. 'You've told us all there is to tell,' he said firmly. 'For the last two days, that's all you've talked about. Savage. His guns.' He shook his head when the boy started to argue. 'No more, Josh,' he said sternly. His gaze shifted to the boy's lunch pail.

'Joshua.' Sarah's voice again, impatient. There was a *spur-r-rongg* as she opened the screen door and waited. Josh stood up, grabbing his lunch tin and his books. Feeling betrayed, he avoided his father's eyes, and – without saying goodbye – stomped across the room and out the door.

He hurried across the yard to the stable. Will was already there, already at his morning chores. He had even saddled Josh's sorrel, ground-hitching her at the corral gate. 'Buck up, Josh!' Will grinned across at his brother, his forehead shiny with sweat. 'Six more weeks, school will be out for the summer!' He reached out, ruffling the younger boy's hair.

Josh pulled away from his brother's touch. *Six weeks, six*

years; it was all the same, he thought. All that wasted time locked up inside the four walls that formed the confines of the one-room schoolhouse. He reached out, hanging his books and lunch box from the strap knotted around the saddle horn, and then pulled himself up on the mare's back.

Will handed him the reins. 'A thanks would have been nice,' he said, nodding at the horse.

Josh grabbed the lines, resentful. 'Nobody asked you to put yourself out,' he growled. He jerked the mare's head around, spiteful, and kicked her into a full run.

He took the shortcut into town, pausing at the fork in the narrow road. The sorrel stopped short, pulled up hard, rearing slightly as she felt the sharp bite of the curb chain. Confused, the animal hesitated, then took a few mincing steps forward toward the familiar path leading to the right, to the schoolhouse. Josh pulled her up short again, see-sawing on the reins as he pulled the mare's head around. It was early yet; he could tell from the sun. If he hurried, he could make it to Harper's office and still be on time for school. Resolutely, he turned the mare to the left, keeping a firm hold on her as they headed toward the main street.

The boardwalks and few concrete sidewalks were almost empty, some of the stores still padlocked and shuttered. The only noise was the steady plodding of the mare, and the natural sounds of early morning. It was the boy's favorite time of day, when the world was fresh and clean, just waking up and coming alive.

He pulled to a halt in front of the doctor's office, throwing his right leg over the saddle horn and slipping lightly to the ground. His boots thudded across the plank walkway, his steps slow, hesitant. He raised his hand to knock on the door, surprised when it opened before he ever touched it.

Harper stepped out into the sunlight, stretching. He gave a quick sweep to his thick mane of gray hair, smoothing it in place and away from his eyes. 'Saw you coming down the street, Josh,' he said yawning. He reached out and slipped a friendly arm around the boy's shoulder. 'You want to know about Savage,' he said, guiding the boy into the gray interior of his office.

Josh grinned up at the man, appreciative. 'Yes, sir,' he replied.

Harper nodded. 'He's back there,' he said, tipping his head toward the door at the end of the room. 'Woke up about five this morning. He's still not sure where he is, or how he got here.' The doctor shook his head, rubbing at a tightness in the back of his neck. 'The man has the constitution of an Apache buck,' he said, the amazement in his voice. 'I didn't give him one chance in hell of pulling through that first night.' Harper saw the impatience in the boy's eyes, and lifted his hand from his shoulder. 'Not too long, Josh,' he cautioned. 'He's still a long way from healed.'

Josh nodded and crossed the room. He opened the door without knocking, raising up on his tiptoes as he entered the sunlit room.

'What the hell...!' Savage bolted upright in the bed, his right hand going to the holster that hung on the bedpost above his left shoulder. He stared into the boy's face for a long time and then relaxed, remembering. He eased the hammer back in place and reholstered the piece, lying back on the pillows.

The kid was thin, too thin, at an age where he was all arms and legs, with the short compact body of a boy who was still growing. His blond hair had already begun to sun-bleach a pale summer-silver in the front, and his cheeks showed the deep red of a beginning tan that set off the blue eyes still filled with the innocence of the very young. 'Dangerous thing, son, coming into a man's room uninvited,' Savage drawled. He tempered the chastisement with a wide grin, exposing a row of fine, white teeth. Gold sparkled from several back fillings. He motioned the youth forward with a

27

wave of his hand. 'You did well, boy, bringing me here,' he said. He nodded at the chair beside the bed.

Josh accepted the unspoken invitation and eased into the chair, unsure of what the man expected. You never knew with grownups, not really. 'Doc said you didn't remember how you got here,' he said. He picked at the edges of his shirt cuff.

Savage nodded. He pointed to the place where his shirt hung, watching as the boy got up and crossed the room. 'Didn't,' he replied. He reached out and took the shirt, digging into the pocket for a long, black-papered cheroot. 'Then I saw your face, that thatch of yellow hair. I knew right off you were the one.' The man searched his other pocket for a match and swore, tossing the shirt aside.

Josh was still on his feet. He pulled a sulfur-tipped match from the front pocket of his denims, biting his bottom lip as he scraped the top with this thumb nail. He tried to hide the smile when the stick snapped and flared a blue-orange flame on the first try. Cupping the match in his hand, he offered Savage a light.

The man mumbled his thanks, taking a long drag on the cigar. He grinned up at the boy, exhaling the foul-smelling smoke. 'They keep telling me that these things are going to kill me.' He shook his head. 'This is the only thing besides a woman and good bottle of Irish whiskey that makes me feel worth a damn!' He laughed at his own joke, an expansive laugh that came from deep in his chest.

'Old Three-Toes, Mr Savage.' Josh had forgotten the match until it burned down to his thumb. Embarrassed, he dropped it on the floor, making a fist around his tender thumb tip.

Savage's brow knotted, and he blew a long series of smoke rings, one inside the other. 'Three-Toes?' he echoed.

Josh turned the chair around and straddled it, his arms folded across the back. 'The old wolf,' he said. 'The cave was his den.'

The bounty hunter surveyed the boy through the blue-gray

smoke. He studied the tip of his smoldering cigar for a time as if thinking, trying to remember. A small smile tugged at the corner of his mouth. *Why not?* he thought, reluctant to lose the boy's company. It had been a long time since he'd seen another human face up close, and even longer since he'd seen one so eager; so innocent and trusting. Nothing but greasers and saloon whores since he had left Texas. After a time, he had even stopped talking to himself. 'Mean,' he said finally. 'God awful mean.' Out of the corner of his eye, he could see the kid's face, and knew that he had the boy's undivided attention.

Jake Kincaid sat at his desk, a mug of cold coffee at his elbow, a bottle of warm rotgut directly in front of him. He debated for at time and then decided on a compromise, pouring a healthy shot of liquor into his cup. Tolerable, he mused, tasting the brew. One part piss poor coffee to an equal part of piss poor whiskey. Considering his disposition, it was a fitting breakfast.

He was in a foul mood; had been, ever since he had recognized Savage. Just thinking of the man tied his guts in knots. All the old fears, the old nightmares, came back to haunt him. All of the old what ifs ... 'Shit!' Kincaid spoke the curse aloud, vehemently, unable to take any solace from the word. He raked the fingers of his left hand through his hair, his right still wrapped about the tin cup, and swore again. '*Shit!*'

One by one, he began to leaf through the thick stack of yellowed flyers on his desk. Pinkerton sheets, with their precise, detailed descriptions. *White male, aged 35 to 40, five feet seven inches, one hundred eighty pounds; top of little finger missing, right hand, knife scar, left forearm.* The lawman wet his thumb and went on to the next sheet, and the next. He lifted each one, studied it, and then turned it face down at his elbow. The flyers were old, too old. The majority of the papers had taken more than a month arriving from the offices in Phoenix.

Kincaid gave the stack of paper a shove, wiping them from his desk with a single vicious sweep of his forearm. They rattled, suspended in the still air, and then drifted to the floor. He sat there for a time, staring at the pile of litter, his fingers teepeed in front of his nose. Nothing. Not one damned thing that was of any use. The lawman exhaled, his breath whistling through his fingers. There had to be a way. Somehow, one way or another, there had to be a way to get rid of Savage.

Now.

CHAPTER 3

'He had me down, son.' Savage lifted his hand, his thumb and forefinger measuring a space so small a piece of paper would not pass between them. 'Had his teeth this far from my gullet.' He shook his head, grimacing, and rubbed at his throat. 'I drew the pistol then.' He cast a covert look at the boy and saw that his lie was believed, and continued, 'I could feel his breath on my cheek, all hot, smelling like blood.' He grinned at that, inwardly pleased with his narrative, more pleased with the look of unabashed awe that spread across the boy's countenance. 'And that's how it was,' he finished. He was on his second cigar when he ended the fairy-tale account of how he had slain the old wolf. Cautious, he cast a sidewise glance at the boy, amused at what he still saw in the kid's face.

'I knew it!' Josh breathed. He shifted in the chair, his chin resting on his arms. 'I knew he'd never give up the cave without a fight!' The boy's face opened up in a wide grin, and his cheeks reddened. 'I thought you were a bear, first time I saw you. That buffalo coat all brown and black, wooled up over your head!'

'Lucky for me I wasn't!' Savage reached out, his fingers touching the boy's arm. 'That old wolf would have torn the hide right off a grizzly, the fight he put up. Why, if I hadn't worked my gun free when I did' – his face became serious –

31

'Doc would have been working on me in the back room, measuring me for a pine overcoat!' He grew silent a moment, reflective. 'I suppose the local law knows I'm here,' he speculated.

'Doc kicked him out,' Josh volunteered. From far in the distance, there sounded a soft, melodious clang of a bell. It failed to reach the boy's ears. 'Uncle Jake said he didn't have no papers on you, so Doc just told him to get out.'

'Uncle Jake?' Savage's interest in the boy had begun to wane, the ache in his chest returning, but now, with this sudden revelation. . . . 'Your uncle the deputy?' he probed.

Josh shook his head. 'Naw,' he answered. 'Jake's the town marshal. Only law, really, this part of the county, what with old man Lathrop in Phoenix most of the time.' There was a strange mixture of pride and embarrassment in the kid's voice as he talked. 'Jake lives with us,' he continued. 'At the ranch. Him and Pa are partners . . .' The boy's words drifted off, his interest shifting to the silverfish that was crawling across the corner of the bed sheet.

Part-time marshal, Savage mused. That meant that the town was either too poor or too quiet to need a full time lawman. The man grinned. Couldn't hurt, staying friendly with the kid. Not as rewarding as the time in Taos when he was romancing the sheriff's daughter, but just as useful. He stuck out his hand, man-to-man. 'I can't keep calling you *boy*, son. You know my name; only seems fair and proper I know yours.'

Josh wiped his hand on his pant leg and accepted Savage's gesture. 'Kincaid,' he said. 'Joshua Kincaid.' He couldn't keep his eyes off the man's fingers.

There was a soft knock at the door, and Savage quickly withdrew his hand, grabbing the LeMat. 'Come!' he called, gesturing for the boy to move away from the bed.

Harper stepped into the room. It was as if he didn't see the pistol. He reached out, taking Savage's cigar. 'I don't much give a damn what you do once you leave here, Savage, but as long as you're in my care . . .' He crushed out the stogie in the wash basin beside the bed.

The bounty hunter protested loudly, jamming the LeMat back into the holster as he rose up from the bed. He bent forward, intent on salvaging the ruined smoke. The coughing began then, simultaneously with the man's sudden forward movement, the bed shaking as he began to whoop violently. There was a harsh, hacking sound, deep down in this chest.

Harper cursed, whacking Savage soundly between his broad shoulders. He grabbed the basin from the bedside table and shoved it under the man's chin. The porcelain bowl began to fill with thick, yellow-brown phlegm tinged with streaks of bright red. The physician turned to the boy. 'Jake is out there.' He jerked his head toward the door. 'You tell him,' he said, his voice rising above the noise of the other man's tortured coughing, 'you tell him that Savage has had all the company he's going to have today.'

Josh stumbled out of his chair, his face white. He'd never been around anyone who was sick. Savage's body was contorted by the convulsive heaving of his chest, his heavy shoulders lifting with each wave of coughing. There was more blood in the basin now; dark at first, then bright red, streaking the man's vomit. The boy retreated from the sickroom, his stomach tied in tight knots. He eased the door shut, still able to hear the loud wheezing as Savage continued to fight for air.

Jake Kincaid was at the far window. He heard the door snap shut and turned to face it. He was expecting Harper, but there was no real surprise in his face when he saw his nephew. He'd seen the sorrel tethered out front. 'Just what the hell do you think you're doing here, boy?' he demanded.

Josh answered the man with a small shrug and jammed his hands deep into his pockets.

The elder Kincaid made a long ceremony out of digging

his watch from his vest pocket. He cupped the timepiece in his hand, still facing the boy. His fingernail tapped the crystal as he held it up for the boy's inspection. 'Eight minutes after ten, Josh,' he said pleasantly. 'Now, if the calendar I got locked in my head isn't all screwed up' – his voice was changing, becoming sarcastic – 'and this thing is right' he turned the watch so it faced the boy – 'it's Monday morning, and you're damn near two hours late for school.'

Damn you! Josh felt the heat of his own blood coloring his face. 'I forgot,' he mumbled, shifting his eyes from the watch to the toes of his boots. Even without seeing it, he could hear the damn thing ticking.

Kincaid's shoulders rose, then fell, and he exhaled loudly. 'Hell, boy,' he breathed, 'the way you've been behaving lately, you'd forget your head if it wasn't tacked on.'

The kid's head snapped up. He knew from his uncle's face that the man was talking about the poorly repaired pen and the dead calf. He squared his shoulders. 'Doc said to tell you that Mr Savage has had all the callers he's going to have. Leastwise, today.' He spun on his heel, and marched toward the door.

The lawman swore. He snapped the face of the watch closed, his knuckles white. For a long time, he stared at the closed door to the adjoining room, his fingers resting on the butt of his gun. The sound of Savage's deep coughing had ceased, and Kincaid found himself hoping the man had died.

The family was already at supper when Jake rode into the yard. He could see Josh's mare in the corral, the animal's back still wet, the outline of a saddle wet-blood dark against her hide. He wondered if the kid had ever made it to school, and then pushed the thought from his mind.

He stabled the bay, and then trudged across the yard to the house, taking the steps one at a time as he headed for the kitchen door. He pulled open the screen, nodding in greeting, smiling in weary gratitude as Sarah went to the stove and took his plate from the warmer. He took his place at the table, directly across from Josh, annoyed when the boy failed to acknowledge his greeting.

The meal progressed with an air of normalcy, the family sharing a quiet, good-natured conversation. Except for Josh. He was silent, his eyes on his plate, sullen. Then, as the setting sun began to stream through the multipaned windows, the boy began making shadow pictures on the white-washed wall at his back, his attention on the baby. 'Carrie,' he called softly. The sulkiness smoothed from his mouth as the little girl clapped her hands and smiled her two-teeth smile. He made them all for her. A rabbit, a long-necked goose, a bird with flapping wings. Finally, the child's favorite: a long-eared horse that moved its mouth as if talking. The child responded with a giggle and clapping hands. Sometimes, Josh observed, it was like Carrie was the only one who really gave a damn about him, paid any attention. He watched as his mother wiped the child's face and lifted her from the highchair. The toddler waved a fat fist at him, the china-blue eyes smiling as she was carried down the hall to her parents' bedroom.

Will excused himself. He was heading out the door when Josh decided it would be wise to join him. He shoved himself away from the table, intent on rising, and felt his father's eyes on him.

J.T. put down his cup. 'Your mother tells me you forgot the wood box this morning,' he said quietly. Again, he thought to himself. He continued, aloud, 'And it seems you've forgotten your manners as well.'

Josh dropped his head. He mumbled a quiet apology. 'Sorry, Pa.' It wasn't enough. He could see it in his father's eyes. 'I'll get the kindling,' he sighed. He looked up, rising, and felt his uncle's eyes on him: judgmental, disapproving. It was as if the man were waiting for him to say something. Excusing himself, the boy left the table, and hurried outside.

*

The two men were on the porch, sharing their customary evening smoke, leaving Sarah the privacy of the house so that she was free to nurse the baby in the comfort of the kitchen. Jake was seated on the porch railing, his back against the corner post, an unlit cigarette clenched between his teeth. 'Harper hasn't let me in to see him.' He stared off at the distant hills, toward town. 'I spent all morning and most of this afternoon, going through the flyers, digging back.' He shook his head, disgusted. 'Nothing!' he declared. 'I couldn't find a damned thing.'

J.T. pulled out his pipe, using his pocket knife to scrape out the bowl. 'Savage always stayed well within the law.' He tapped the pipe on the porch railing, and then carefully filled the bowl. 'It's been a lot of years, Jake. You've got no way of knowing why he's here, or even if this is where he was headed.'

'Yeah.' Jake's cigarette bobbed as he spoke. He faced his brother. 'I just don't want to take any chances, J.T. I don't want it to be like it was before.' He slammed a clenched fist against the railing, his jaws tight. 'Twenty years,' he said, more to himself than the other. 'Twenty years, and I'll lay odds he's still looking to get even.'

J.T. lowered his head, cupping his hand against the evening breeze as he lit his pipe. He sucked hard, getting a good start, the pleasant scent of apple-mellowed tobacco filling the air around them. 'No sense borrowing trouble, Jake,' he said softly, his eyes on his brother.

'I don't plan on borrowin' it,' Jake replied, 'but I don't figure on not being ready if it comes.' His voice lowered. 'I keep remembering Savage like he was then. A peacock; a strutting peacock. Never a hair out of place, his fingernails clean and barbershop trimmed.

'And those damned white shirts.' The lawman shook his head. He took the cigarette from his mouth, rolling it between his thumb and forefinger, the tobacco sifting on to the porch floor. 'Everything just so, picture book pretty. No flaws, no imperfections, even the way he spoke.' He was quiet a long moment, remembering. More than once, he had heard women comparing Savage to the brooding and darkly handsome Edwin Booth. 'He's lame, J.T.,' he murmured. 'That leg was busted up real bad back then, and it's stiff now, stiff as a board and a good half-inch shorter than the other. Man like Savage could find that hard to live with. Real hard.' The silence was there again, the man playing with the still unlit smoke. 'Josh was at Harper's today,' he said. 'He was there to see Savage. To talk to him.'

J.T. lifted his head, interested. 'Before school?' he asked.

'Before and during,' the other answered. 'He was still there at ten o'clock.' His fingers drifted to his watch pocket as he remembered.

J.T. studied his brother's profile, reading the worry. 'Josh is like any other kid in town,' he observed. 'There isn't a boy who can read, hasn't read something about Savage, one time or another. Buntline wrote about him almost as much as he did about Earp, and just about as truthful.

'It will pass, Jake. It will all pass.'

The elder Kincaid faced his brother fully. It was as if he hadn't heard the man's words, or understood his reasoning. 'I don't think it's a good thing for Josh to be around Savage, to talk to him. To listen to him.'

J.T. stared across the yard to where his younger son was diligently working at the wood pile. 'Josh is a dreamer, Jake. He sees a thing, admires it for awhile, and then goes on to something else. It'll be the same with Savage.' He reached out, slipping his arm around his brother's shoulder in an affectionate squeeze. 'You'll see, Jake. This isn't any different from the first time a boy falls in love. It will take all his time for a while, all his attention. And then he'll wake up one morning, and there'll be some other, more interesting thing wiggling a come-here finger at him, and Savage will be forgotten.'

Jake mulled over his brother's words, knowing from the man's tone that he didn't really believe what he was saying. 'I hope so, J.T.,' he said fervently. 'I sure in hell hope so.'

They were in the schoolyard, eating lunch, hunkered down in the sparse shade of the budding palo verde trees. 'You're full of crap, Josh!' Clell Avery snorted. 'My old man said that Savage ain't no better than some kill-from-behind bush-whacker!' He tore the book Josh had been reading from the boy's hands. 'And this stuff is just so much horse crap, too.'

Immediately, Josh was on his feet. He grabbed for the book the older boy had snatched from his hands. 'Yeah? Well, I've talked to Savage.' He waved the magazine under Avery's nose. 'He said it's true. All of it!'

The older boy laughed. 'Sure! And then he told you all about Santy Claus and Mother Goose!' Avery shrieked, almost doubling over in laughter, his voice cracking.

Josh yielded to his temper, goaded by the infectious laugh-ter of the other boys who were gathered around them. He knotted a fist and took a punch at the side of Avery's head.

'All right, gentlemen.' Clara Altman was at the front door to the schoolhouse, her eyes on the clutch of youths at the foot of the steps. 'I think that's quite enough.' She turned her attention from the two combatants, clapping her hands sharply twice, summoning the other students from the play yard.

She reached out as Josh came up the stairs, her right hand extended. 'I'll take the book, Joshua,' she said quietly. Her brow furrowed, and she shook her head, her eyes scanning the gaudy cover. Josh lowered his head. Behind him, he could still hear Clell's mocking laughter.

They filed to their assigned seats, the smaller children at the long benches in the front rows, the older students taking the tables at the rear. The girls were on the left side of the

room, properly starched and combed. On the right were the
boys, dusty kneed from their noontime games and combat.

Josh flopped down into his seat, wishing himself somewhere else. It had been a week since he'd brought Savage into
town. He had spent as much time as he could with the man,
going to Harper's office immediately after school. There was
only so much time he could spend with the bounty hunter
and still escape getting into trouble at home, but so far, he
had managed.

He ran the man's errands, tended his horse. And they
talked. Man to man; about everything, even the scars that
marred the man's body. A knife wound, almost eight inches
long on the man's back and right shoulder. 'Apache, Josh,'
Savage had explained. 'Half-breed, cut from the same tree as
Rufus Buck and his wild bunch. He raped a twelve-year-old
white girl. Made her mother and father watch, then cut her
throat and took her scalp.'

There were bullet wounds, too. A shallow indentation in
his shoulder incurred during a running gun battle with a
forty-year old lawman who had gone bad, and a finger-wide
crease at the hairline above his right ear. Savage had laughed
heartily when he told Josh about that wound, his voice secretive, and his dark eyes dancing. 'A whore, Josh!' he had whispered, pulling himself up on one elbow as he fingered the
spot. 'She got wind I was looking for some cowboy she was
partial to. Cool as ice, that one. Set me on fire with her
fingers, got me going just fine and then ... bang!' The
bounty man laughed at the double meaning, remembering
his peaked passions. 'She pulled this little pearl-handled
derringer and tries her damnedest to blow my head off!' He
sank back on the pillow then, scratching at a place beneath
the blankets. 'Couldn't hear for a month of Sundays,' he
said, and there wasn't one hint of regret or remorse in his
words.

The catalogue of injuries was endless, like the long list of

39

towns and cities where the little wars had occurred. Phoenix, El Paso, Kansas City, Deadwood, San Francisco, New Orleans. Magic names that were just places on a map to a kid who had never been any more than twenty miles from home.

The leg wound was the one that had intrigued Josh the most. He had a brief glimpse of the injury when the big man shifted in the bed, averting his eyes when he knew from Savage's face and actions that the tangled white scar was a source of discomfort and embarrassment for the man. 'Kilkenny,' Savage murmured, in answer to the boy's unasked question. He massaged the stiff joint, his eyes on the far wall. 'Jason Kilkenny. The only one who ever got away from me.' The man's tone was at once fierce and almost reverent. 'Shot me from ambush. Smashed my knee and left me to bleed to death; stuck beneath a dead horse.' Savage recited the story without looking at the boy, his voice whisper quiet and filled with rage. 'He shot my horse out from under me, and left me to rot.

'Food for the birds,' he finished. A raw hatred filled his words. 'Food for the birds.'

Josh shifted in his seat, goaded back to reality by the hardness of the wooden bench.

It was getting hot inside the schoolroom, unbearably hot. He could hear Miss Altman's voice droning in the background, steady, hypnotic, like the noise of the bees outside the open window. Only the bees were far more interesting.

He took out his pad of unruled paper and began sketching, his pencil making soft, sweeping sounds on the stiff paper. His mind drifted as he worked, and he saw the drawing through an artist's eyes. Imperfections in the rough manila paper began to form patterns beneath the soft-leaded pencil; a knothole in a board fence . . . a wispy piece of grass poking out from the framework of a warped and uneven boardwalk. Josh stole two quick looks at the front of the room, tracing the form of Clara Altman with hurried, swift strokes, exaggerating her small breasts and tiny, corseted waist. She was the horrified onlooker he needed to add to the drama in his scenario, and he drew her with her hand over her mouth, as if she were about to scream. Grinning, Josh added a pair of wire-framed spectacles, purposely unflattering to the plain but well-proportioned face. He was pleased with the likeness, and paused to shade her cheeks with his fingers.

Then the sketching resumed. Bold, heavy strokes, the boy intent on his creation.

A shadow appeared across the desk, crawling across the pages of Josh's open tablet. 'Very interesting, Joshua . . . and so graphic.' A slim white hand reached down, picking up the thick pad. 'However, it's not quite what I asked you to do.' She nodded at the blackboard behind her desk.

Josh followed the woman's gaze and saw the unsolved mathematical problem, his face coloring as he heard the high-pitched twittering of the girls, and the more boisterous laughter of the older boys. The woman raised her hand and her right eyebrow in unison, and the sound died a sudden death. She studied the picture, pleased with the boy's ability if not his subject matter. A reasonably good representation of herself, and the detailed likeness of a man holding a smoking gun. He faced a half-finished figure of another man, also armed; a man who had obviously been shot. A boy's parody of an illustration from a cheap dime novel.

'Your Mr Savage, I presume.' She tore the sheet from the tablet, folding it into precise quarters. 'You'll remain after school, Joshua. Perhaps then you'll be able to keep your mind on your studies, and complete your assigned work.'

Josh swallowed. He looked up at the woman, angry. He had plans; elaborate plans to help Savage move from Doc Harper's to a room over Fulton's Saloon. He had even created an intricate tapestry of lies to explain to his parents why he wouldn't be home until just before supper, and the lies had been believed. 'No!' he said loudly.

41

Miss Altman has already started down the aisle toward the front of the room. She turned, canting her head. 'I beg your pardon.' Her voice was deceptively soft.

Josh could feel the eyes on him; all the eyes. He exchanged a heated glance with the snickering Clell Avery, seeing the scorn in the other boy's eyes. 'No!' he repeated. 'I won't stay after school!'

The woman turned her back on the boy and went to her desk. The murmur of many voices followed her, and she tapped on the desk with her long ruler. Without looking at Josh, she began reciting the homework assignments for the younger children, then did the same for the other sections. The Regulator clock on the far wall seemed to be ticking in perfect synchronization with her instructions. Finished, she took off her glasses. 'You may all leave now,' she said, and the large hand on the clock jumped to the half-hour mark. Precisely three-thirty. She nodded at each row in proper sequence, calling out the numbers. 'Row 5, please,' she said finally. Everyone stood up, including Josh, and – single file – started toward the door.

Josh was the last one in his line. He headed toward the outer door, and found his way blocked by the woman. 'Sit down, Joshua,' she ordered. She pointed to the chair beside her desk.

A shadow lingered in the doorway, and Josh knew who it was. He could hear the muffled laughter of Clell Avery and another. They were waiting, watching to see what Josh would do, how he would deal with the woman. 'No!' Josh dropped his head, avoiding the woman's eyes. He had loved her when he was little – would have died for her. And then she started seeing his uncle, and everything had changed. 'No,' he breathed. He brushed by her, pushing her aside when she attempted to stop him. He paused at the door just long enough to plant a well-aimed fist in the middle of Clell Avery's soft belly.

He didn't head for home. He mounted the sorrel and rode

directly into town. Eyes staring straight ahead, he trotted past the jail, ignoring the chill at his back as he passed his uncle's office.

CHAPTER 4

They were unpacking the last of Savage's belongings, Josh watching as the man limped back and forth across the room from the bed to the dresser. The bounty-man's saddle-bags had been packed full. Josh had wondered at their bulk and weight when he carted them from the livery. Now he watched as the man spread his belongings on the white bedspread.

Clothing, mostly. A dark suit of good quality, two vests, and several white shirts. These were carefully wrapped in blue paper, starched and laundered. Savage saw the look on the boy's face. He grinned, and reached into his leather pouch for a coin. 'I want you to fetch me a barber, Josh. Not some ordinary hair-butcher, but one who knows how to give a good shave and a proper haircut.' He flipped a coin into the air, watching as the boy instinctively reached out for the gleaming bit of gold. 'Yours,' he said. He tossed the youth another. 'You tell the barber that one is his, and there will be another one when he's done.'

There was a knock at the door, a light tap-tap. Savage answered, as if he were expecting the unseen caller. He opened the door wide, bowing slightly. And then he stood back, watching the movement of the woman's hips as she came into the room. She was carrying a stack of clean towels, and the two Mexicans with her were struggling with a dented copper tub. Savage turned to Josh, winking. He gave a single nod in the woman's direction. 'You take your time finding that barber, Josh,' he said.

Josh waited for a good two hours before he returned with the barber in tow, not sure if he had allowed too much time or too little. He remembered to knock and call out before entering.

Savage was in the tub. There was steam rising from the water, and the bounty hunter lounged back against the sloped metal rim. He had a silver flask in one hand, and a large water tumbler in the other. There was a scent in the air; lilac water, and something else. Something salty; briny. Josh had noticed the odor right off, and somehow – without knowing what it was – found that it pleasured him.

The girl who was scrubbing Savage's back pleased him even more. She was young; younger than the woman who had first come into the room, younger still than the other women he had seen congregated in the bar when he had come up the stairs. Same age as Will, he reckoned; eighteen, maybe nineteen, and soft in all the right places. There was something ceremonious in the way she was bathing the man in the tub, her movements rhythmic, sure. She stood up to make room for the barber and went to the foot of the tub.

Josh almost fell over his own feet backing away when she crossed in front of him. She was naked. Or at least as damned close as she could come. Her legs seemed to go on forever, leading to a trim waist, and her bare arms and shoulder. . . . Josh swallowed; hard. He'd seen pictures; he and Will had snuck a look at the thin cardboard lithographs that came in the packs of ready-rolled cigarettes his uncle sometimes purchased at the general store. But this . . . this beat the living hell out of any picture!

'You look like you could use a drink, son!' Savage waved the youth forward. He handed him the flask of whiskey, nodding his head. 'Just take it slow, Josh,' he instructed paternally. 'It'll burn like fires of Hell the first time,' he laughed,

45

leaning forward to caress the girl's exposed thigh, 'but then it will feel just fine.'

What the man said was true. The first swallow did burn going down. But the second one was better, and the one after that . . . that one made Josh feel warm in places he didn't know he had.

So did the girl. The longer he looked at her – and he could not stop looking at her – the warmer he felt.

When the barber was finished, Savage called for a blanket, draping the cloth around his shoulders before standing up. Stepping out of the tub, he kept his back to the others, and disappeared behind the fabric covered screen in the corner. Item by item, the clothing disappeared from the rack where Savage had hung them out for brushing: the trim-fitting gray trousers, the immaculately starched white shirt, the black silk tie. Finally, the man stepped from behind the screen.

Josh was surprised at the transformation. Immaculate, his beard and hair neatly trimmed, Savage had the look of a member of the landed gentry. The man paid the barber, then pulled the girl to him, pressing a gold coin into her hand as he whispered into her ear. She nodded her head, and padded across the room, laughing.

Savage was in an expansive mood. He finished combing his hair, watching the boy's distorted reflection in the oval mirror above the dresser. 'Do you want her?' he asked.

Josh stared at the man's mirrored image, puzzled. He could see the girl reflected in the glass, see her as she sprawled across the bed. He averted his eyes and took another long drink from the bottle, tilting his head far back. When he finished, his head came forward, and his eyes were locked on the mirror. On the girl's reflection.

She was lounging on the bed, cat-like, propped up on one side in such a way that her breasts were pushed together. They were like twin ivory mountains, spilling from the cotton camisole she was wearing, the valley between them tightly closed by her posture. She lifted a hand to her throat, trailing tiny red lines on her skin with her nails, beginning at a place beneath her chin. The scarlet paths led downward, closer and closer to the narrow division between the mounds.

Josh watched, entranced. He took another lingering pull on the bottle, his lips locked in place around the narrow opening as he sucked the whiskey deep into his throat. There was no warm burn in his mouth this time, just a numbness on his gums and lips. He couldn't seem to take his eyes of the girl. There was a strange feeling in his crotch. The whiskey-warmth seemed to have settled there, and it was growing.

Savage watched the boy, watched as the girl subtly enticed him. The kid was green; too green. By this time in his own life, he had screwed his way through most of the bordellos in New Orleans, and was starting on a second go-round. *This is no way to raise a boy*, he mused, *keeping him penned up and away from things that are as natural as flood and famine.* He reached out, tugging at the kid's sleeve. 'Take her,' he ordered, knowing in all likelihood that it would be the girl who did the taking the first time around. He nodded at the bed, studying the boy's profile, and could see that the kid was torn by some inner argument. *The little fool thinks he will burn in Hell for this!* Gingerly, with the back of his hand, Savage tapped the front of the boy's trousers. 'It isn't any great sin, son. You'll go to Hell twice as quick, throwing it away behind the barn.' He saw from the sudden color in the boy's cheeks that he had guessed right. 'What you want,' he said softly, his hand on the boy's arm, 'isn't any more wrong than taking a healthy leak.' He smiled when the boy turned to face him. 'Just as natural,' he cajoled. 'A lot more fun, but just as much relief.' He slapped the boy's shoulder. 'Supper,' he said, changing the subject. 'I'm going to get me some supper.' He turned on his heel, and ushered the barber into the hall.

Josh heard the door close. The hair on the back of his neck seemed to stand straight up, as coarse as the hair on a wild

47

boar's back. He felt light-headed; giddy. The whiskey had begun to work on him; the whiskey and the girl.

He had never felt like this. Not once in all his life. A thousand things raced through his mind; a thousand fantasies. Unable to stop himself, he laughed aloud, not understanding why.

The girl joined him, her laughter low, sensual, coming from deep within. Josh faced her, biting his lower lip as she sat up on the bed and began to remove her camisole; slowly, her fingers unlacing the faded blue satin ribbon that held the fragile cloth in place. She undid the top three laces and then stopped, leaning forward to waggle a single, slim finger at the boy.

The bottle Josh held in his hand slipped from his fingers and thumped on to the braided rug at the foot of the bed. He stood there, aware of the tightness at his crotch, his belly filling with a pleasant dull ache that begged for release. He crossed the few feet to the bed and reached out, his hand hovering above the girl's breasts. Then he touched her.

The girl pulled herself upright, her arms tight around Josh's neck. She kissed him, on the cheek first, her laughter warm and moist against his neck. Josh returned the kiss, leaning forward. He was clumsy, kissing her on the mouth the way he had kissed his mother goodnight for as long as he could remember.

The returned kiss was not maternal. The girl pulled at Josh, coaxing him over the brass frame at the foot of the bed. They collapsed into the covers, their arms entwined. He felt the heat of the girl's tongue against his teeth, a shiver running through him as she ran her tongue across his upper lip. He opened his mouth to inhale, only to have it filled with the girl's tongue.

Momentarily repulsed, he tried to draw away. And then he found himself unable to pull his mouth from hers, and they kissed again. It was . . . Josh didn't know; didn't care. They undressed each other. What had begun as a joke – a folly – for the girl, became a passion of mutual curiosity. The girl had been used many times before; badly, and usually in a great hurry by cowhands who really didn't give a damn about her needs. The boy was different. His movements were cautious, gentle. As if he were afraid she would disappear and no longer be there beside him.

Eventually Josh rolled off the girl, welcoming the feel of the sudden coolness of the mattress at his back. He was at once exhausted and completely exhilarated.

The girl sat up, searching among the blankets for her clothing. Her hand disappeared beneath the coverlet, and she laughed, withdrawing the bottom half of the boy's longjohns. They dressed in silence, suddenly shy at their nakedness, their backs to each other. Josh felt the girl's fingers on his neck, and he leaned into her touch. 'Leona,' she said, working the curl at his ear between her fingers. '*Mi nombre es Leona.*' She was quiet again, stroking his neck. 'I want you to come again, boy.' She laughed, muffling the sound with her closed hand as she realized the double meaning in her words. It was no lie. 'You hear me, boy?'

Josh turned, his face flushed. 'I hear.' He nodded at the bed. 'It was all right,' he said gallantly, and the words almost sounded like a question.

'More than all right,' the girl replied, tossing her head. She reached up, sweeping her long hair away from her face. 'You come back sometime,' she cast a fleeting look at Josh and then dropped her eyes, suddenly ashamed. 'It won't cost,' she said quietly.

Josh nodded. He didn't care if it did.

CHAPTER 5

Savage had finished his supper. He shoved back his chair, using a wooden match for a toothpick, his eyes busy cataloging faces within the room. Ranchers, mostly; a few dirt farmers in their flat-soled work shoes and full-body coveralls. Reasonably prosperous looking for the most part, farmer and cattleman alike. The bounty hunter grinned. It was a Friday night crowd in search of Friday night release, and the noise of silver coins and clinking glasses rang loud above the sound of their jumbled conversations.

The barmaid approached the table, carrying a full bottle and two reasonably clean glasses. She shoved aside the litter and sat down, leaning forward as she worked the cork out of the green bottle. 'Thought you might like some company with this, Mr Savage,' she smiled.

Savage ignored the woman's presence, chewing on the toothpick as if he were deep in thought. Then he spoke, staring past the woman to the stairs. 'I have all the company I need,' he said flatly. 'Younger, and not all used up.' He was thinking of the girl upstairs, and the money he had given her to wait for him.

Incensed, the woman started to protest. The argument died on her lips as she followed the gunman's gaze. Contemptuously, she tossed her head, her eyes narrowing as she watched the young boy come down the stairway. Her smile was a tight, red line across a pinched face. 'This isn't any pig farm, Savage,' she hissed. She started to rise. 'Been a long time since I was turned down in favor of some smooth-cheeked boy.'

Savage backhanded her, a vicious blow that brought tears. He came forward in his seat at the same time. 'You watch your mouth, woman.' He smiled then, easing back in the chair, his eyes ice. Reaching into his vest pocket, he took out a silver dollar. 'Go buy yourself a cowboy,' he sneered.

The whore was on her knees. She wiped the corner of her mouth with the back of her right hand, picking up the coin with her left. Sobbing, she rose up from the floor, and headed toward the bar. In her flight, she brushed past Josh, pausing just long enough to rake him with a long, menacing stare.

Savage pushed out a chair with his good leg. He poured the boy a drink and shoved the glass across the table. 'She said something about telling your uncle that you were here,' the man lied.

Josh sat. He cast a furtive glance at the woman. The worry was real. 'She—'

'Won't say anything now,' Savage finished for the boy. He tapped the rim of Josh's shot glass with his finger, smiling across at the youth. 'You don't look any the worse for the wear,' he observed. 'And it doesn't appear that God was of a mind to strike you dead for your trespasses.'

Josh felt himself coloring, his cheeks warm. 'Ma says that God is too busy to bother with this kind of trash. . . .' He waved his arm in an ambiguous gesture toward the crowded room, and took a drink. The whiskey warmed him again, burning its way down his throat. 'I figure that makes Him too busy to look for me!'

Savage laughed. He pointed to the plates in the middle of the table. 'You hungry, boy?'

Josh shook his head. 'It was like you said, Mr Savage.' He took another drink, thinking of the girl and the time they had spent together. 'Just like you said,' he repeated.

Savage stood up and gestured for the boy to do the same. He looped a fatherly arm around the kid's shoulder, enjoying the game. 'Hell, son, I've got no reason to lie to you.' He led the youth away from the table. 'You ever play poker, Josh? I hear they've got a small game going in Greasetown.'

Josh was aware of the way the crowd was eyeing Savage; the way they moved aside as the man passed. 'No, sir,' he answered. The floor seemed to rise up to meet him, and he paused in his walking, half-turning to stare fully at Savage.

He was surprised to see that the man was unarmed; dressed like a Phoenix dude and not wearing one weapon. Savage saw the look, the question in the boy's eyes. 'First night out in a strange town, Josh. You never – *never* – show your hand in a strange town; not until you get a feel for the place, for the people.' They were out the door now, on the wide boardwalk. Savage continued talking, his arm still on the boy's shoulder. 'You pick a quiet place, away from the regular townsfolk. Find a table in a far corner, sit with your back to the wall. Play a little cards, drink a little whiskey. Talk to the ladies.' Their boots thunked hollowly on the walkway, the sound different as they headed down the three steps into the dirt street. Josh was feeling light-headed; light-headed and full grown. 'Town rules and trail rules,' Savage was saying.

'In town, you watch the people; the law. On the trail, you ride a dark horse – a light-colored one makes an easy target – and you never cast a big shadow.' The man led the way across the street, heading toward the *lamparas* that lit the pathway leading to the line of rundown cantinas. 'That way, Josh, you stay alive. Because, if you follow all the rules, all the time, you get the man before he gets you.' Savage's mood changed suddenly, his hand going briefly to his lame knee, and then he was silent.

They picked the larger of the two *cantinas* on the south side of the street, following the sound of the *mariachis*. Savage led the boy into the long narrow room, pausing in the doorway as his eyes adjusted to the dim lights that hung above the mirror-less bar. The music faded as the crowd returned the man's quick surveillance, the hushed whispers rising, then diminishing. Making a place for the gunman and his young companion, the men at the bar stood aside, and nodded subdued but guarded greetings.

Savage returned their salutations in flawless border Spanish, his manner friendly, almost solicitous. He pulled out a gold eagle from this vest pocket and laid it on the bar, calling for the barkeep. '*Tragos*,' he said, '*por todos.*' Drinks. For everyone. His offer broke the tension, and the room came alive with laughter, music and the hearty greetings of men ripe for the picking.

Jake Kincaid was whistling, his mood vastly improved. He made his night-time rounds with an air of relaxed joviality, sharing an occasional, raucous greeting with the cowhands he met.

Savage was leaving. That single thought filled the lawman with a gratifying sense of satisfaction and gave him comfort. Doc Harper had given him the news at supper. '*He's leaving, Jake. Said he was going to spend one night making sure everything still functions . . .*' the physician jerked a thumb at his own crotch '*. . . and then he's getting out.*'

Kincaid was visibly relieved. So much so that he changed his mind about a whiskey supper and indulged in a steak and a plate of fried potatoes. A tremendous weight had been lifted from his shoulders, and he felt more at ease than he had in all the long days since Savage had first appeared.

Hell, he mused, trying the lock on the back door of the shuttered mercantile. *The most trouble Savage could get into at the local whorehouse was the kind no lawman would need to mix into.* He grinned. *Rosie*, he thought. *I hope Savage still likes 'em young and well endowed.*

Rosie had the clap.

*

Savage settled in, taking a table in the far corner of the room. Interested, the *vaqueros* began to drift toward the well dressed *gringo* who spoke their language so well. He bantered with them, good-natured and jovial, his deep, rich laughter coming easy.

Josh watched the man; the man and the people in the room. He began to relax, shoving aside the old prejudices and hostilities he had always harbored toward the Mexicans. At ease, he settled into a chair at the gunman's left elbow, watching as the barman scurried to cater to Savage's wants and need. The people – all the people – treated the man with great respect, bowing politely to his requests, then hurrying away to carry them out. A new deck of cards first, the seal unbroken. And then the amber-tinted bottle.

Mescal. Savage explained, pouring the boy a drink. Cautiously, Josh tasted the liquor, the insides of lips burning; his gums feeling like they were on fire. Savage laughed softly, and called for a plate of warm tortillas. 'They'll take away the bite,' he said, 'without dulling the taste.'

Josh sat there, gnawing on the flat bread, sipping the potent liquor. He had forgotten everything; everything except Savage – Savage and the good feeling in his belly when he drank the man's whiskey, and the better feeling at his crotch when he watched the girls who paraded to and from the table.

Savage was playing cards, a large stack of coins in front of him. Josh watched, closing one eye as the cards got blurry, the diamonds and hearts swimming, merging; becoming indistinguishable one from the other. Then he saw that Savage was no longer drinking, and he stopped, too. Except when his stomach grew cold, he found himself craving the warmth.

He saw the girl then. Dark, sensual. *A 'breed,* Josh figured, noting her dusky skin and brilliant black eyes. She had the blackest hair Josh had ever seen, and the light played on it

54

like sun on a raven's wing.

She was old; older than Josh at any rate. At her peak physically, with a small trim waist and generous breasts that seemed to ripple as she walked. She moved among the men at the bar, teasing and joking with them, coquettishly whirling away from their groping hands. Her laughter was a pleasure to a man's ears; soft and melodious.

And her legs. She wore her skirts shorter than most women, well above her ankles, and when she twirled away from the men, the skirt lifted, bright red against the soft, dusky tan of her exposed thighs.

Josh stared at her, unabashed in his admiration. He was thinking again of the little whore in the room at Fulton's; the way she had made him feel. He wanted very much to feel the same thing again, with this girl. Now.

He left the table, pausing to accept the pile of silver dollars Savage knowingly shoved into his palm. He tried to thank the man, and was waved away like a kid in a candy store, unmindful of the shared reminiscences of the older men still playing cards. Their good-natured laughter followed him as he pursued the girl across the room.

His eyes never left her. She moved with the lazy grace of a stalking cat. She would pause, sharing a drink or a secret joke, before moving on, her eyes busy. Her gaze would settle on a man's poke, the stack of coins at his elbow, and then she would move on. Never too long in one place; never too long with one man.

The *mescal* had filled the boy with a bravado that made him exceedingly bold. He sauntered across the room, following after the girl. He caught up with her finally, at the end of the long bar. 'Drink?' he asked.

The girl turned, facing him. A smile pulled at the corner of her mouth, and she raised a wary eyebrow. He was young, so very young. '*Muchacho?*'

The drink had brought the color to Josh's face. He knew

from the woman's expression that she was not taking his offer seriously. Squaring his shoulders, he dug into his pocket. He laid a coin on the bar and, when the woman's face didn't change, followed the first with a second. '*Mescal*,' he said to the barkeep. 'And a glass for the lady.'

The bartender wiped the back of his hand across his mouth, hiding the smile. He nodded, exchanging a quick glance with the woman when he placed the bottle on the bar.

The woman waited as Josh poured them both a drink. She could hear the soft, guttural entreaties of her pimp behind her, and tossed her head in response. Reaching out, she fingered the coins the boy had placed on the bar. 'You have more?' she asked.

Josh stuck his hand in his pocket, the remaining coins Savage had doled out to him during the evening making an agreeable sound. 'Sure,' he said, bragging. 'Lots more.'

The woman nodded, a dimple appearing on her chin as she pursed her lips in approval. 'We could drink here, *chamaco*, or . . .' She canted her head, smiling. Her right shoulder dropped slightly and her blouse slipped even lower. She leaned forward.

Josh swallowed. The woman's breasts were almost fully exposed. They were large, different from the young girl at Fulton's. Softer, more pliant. More abundant. Without thinking, Josh reached out.

The woman laughed, catching his hand mid-air. Holding on, she nodded at the change lying on the bar. 'My house,' she whispered.

Josh grinned. He nodded his acceptance, grabbing the bottle with his free hand. Two women in one night. He rocked back and forth on his toes. *Savage had told him the truth. It sure beat the hell out of hiding in the jake, or out behind the barn. His mother was wrong; they were all wrong. There wasn't a damned thing to be afraid of inside a whorehouse. Not one damned thing.* 'Ma'am,' he said, bowing slightly.

Savage felt a small tug at his elbow. He had just filled out a king high flush, and was anticipating a healthy raise when his turn came. The tug came a second time, more urgently. 'The boy,' the man said, nodding toward the dance floor. Savage looked up, following the Mexican's gaze. Josh was squiring a woman toward the back door.

The bounty hunter spread his cards, flicking the corner of one with the manicured nail of his long index finger. 'The boy just found out that there's more to women than mothers and schoolmarms,' he said in Spanish. He laughed, winking at his companion. 'Now he wants to dance with them all. . . .'

The old Mexican nodded, stroking his chin. 'Not that one,' he said, nodding toward the back door. The woman's pimp and another man had just eased through the opening. 'That one will leave him broken in the alley, with his pockets empty.'

It was a difficult decision for the bounty man to make, sacrificing the first decent hand of the evening in order to follow the boy. He swore angrily, then threw down his cards, and hurried for the back door.

He stepped out into the alley and caught a brief glimpse of two men scurrying in and out between the buildings. Bending forward, he reached down, pulling up the pant leg on his game leg. The knife filled his hand, the rawhide-bound haft reassuring against his palm. Keeping in the shadows, he dogged the two men, playing their game of hide and seek for the length of the alley.

The men disappeared around a corner, Savage behind them. The sound of muffled laughter and Josh's voice brought Savage up short. He flattened against the wall, peering around the corner. The two Mexicans were crouched behind a packing crate, watching Josh and the woman.

Savage surveyed the alley, looking for a vantage place that would keep him hidden and yet give him a clear view of the back door and the *cantina*. He didn't want this; didn't need it. All he had wanted was a nice, quiet evening. A little cards;

some harmless screwing around. And yet here he was, playing daddy to some wet-nosed kid who didn't know a bushwhack from a bull's ass end! The bounty man rolled his shoulders. It was his own fault. He should have watched the kid more closely; watched him, or sent him home.

He darted across the alley and, keeping his back to the wall, worked his way along the adjoining buildings. The narrow passageway came to a dead end, closed off by a high wooden fence. Savage could clearly make out the figures of Josh and the girl, the boy standing with his face to the wall, the woman trapped between his arms. Savage waited until the two men made their move. Then, when they were almost on the boy, he stepped out of his hiding place.

'All right, gentlemen. The party's over.' He tapped the blade of the knife against his belt buckle, still in the shadows, the sound of metal against metal coming like the noise of a pistol being cocked.

'What the heck. . . !' Josh spun around, his face white as he spied the two men.

Savage saw the glint of silver in one of the men's hands and stepped aside as the pimp rushed him. He rewarded the man's efforts with a knee in the groin, and then dropped him, the haft of the knife slapping hard across the Mexican's temple with a loud, dull thud. The second man was already on his way down the alley at a dead run.

Savage stepped out of the shadows, watching as the boy moved away from the woman. She stood there, shivering, her blouse open to the waist. 'Maybe tomorrow,' he said, smiling. 'Maybe you'll have better luck tomorrow.' He touched her cheek, turning the caress into a vicious slap. He took her arm and shoved her down the alley.

Josh watched as Savage emptied the fallen man's pockets, his head still fogged by the liquor he had consumed. He reached out with his foot, toeing the unconscious man. 'What'll we do with him?' he asked.

Savage jingled the handful of coins he had taken from the Mexican, and flipped them to the boy. 'We leave him where he lies,' he said, struggling to stand up. He dusted off his knees. 'Come morning, he'll wake up with a headache; a big headache.' Savage shook his head at the youth. 'The one you would have had, if I hadn't come out here.' He raked the boy with his eyes. 'He could have killed you, son.'

Josh nodded. He brightened then, grinning up at the man. 'She set me up, didn't she?'

'That's right, boy,' Savage answered. He started down the alley.

Josh laughed again, the sound ending in a joyous whoop. He hurried to catch up with the man, touching his sleeve. 'I still think she was worth it,' he breathed, scratching himself. 'Yep! I still think she was worth it!'

Savage roared, touched by the memory of what it was like to be very young, when everything was an adventure. 'Well, you'll never die from a case of the wants, boy; it's the *doing* that can get you killed. . . .' He laughed again, reaching out to box the boy's ears.

They had returned to Fulton's and Savage was teaching Josh the fine art of partnership poker. The boy proved a quick and eager student, flashing the bounty man prearranged signals as he wandered around the card table.

They were in the middle of a six-man game of five-card stud when the cowboy came into the barroom. Josh had a nodding acquaintance with the man, a new rider from the Indian Territory. Nobody knew much about him; just that he did his job, minded his own business, and stayed out of trouble. He did seem to look over his shoulder a lot, but no one cared. It was bad manners to ask a stranger questions, and Josh, like the others, never did.

There was a change in Savage; a subtle, almost imperceptible change. It had begun when the cowboy first entered the room. The bounty hunter pushed the chair away from the table, his eyes on the new arrival. He stood up, waving Josh back into his chair, and walked directly to where the man stood at the bar drinking.

They stood there for a time, Savage and the Oklahoma cowhand, two men exchanging courteous and cautious niceties, as if they were idly passing the time of day. Savage moved to the man's left, his movements insidious, cunning, and placed both of his hands on the bar, in plain sight, away from his waist. Then he ordered a bottle of bourbon. Kentucky bourbon.

The swamper had been watching the pair, pausing in his mopping to scrutinize both men. He knew instinctively what he was seeing, just as the others in the room knew. He dropped his mop and edged out of the batwings, the sound of his flat-heeled shoes fading as he hurried across the plank walkway and down into the street.

Josh rose up from his chair. He stood transfixed, watching Savage. The man hunter was talking, his voice soft and, as he talked, the other men at the bar began to back away. And then there was only Savage, Savage and the young cowhand.

The rider's face went white, and sweat began to bead at his forehead. His hand trembled as he lifted his glass, and the whiskey spilled on his shirt. Savage refilled the man's glass, his own hand steady, his face passive; calm.

The cowboy panicked. He reached out suddenly with this right hand, sweeping the glass from the bar. 'You ain't takin' me, Savage. Goddamn you! *You ain't takin' me back. . . .*' The young man backed up half a step, his hand dropping to his holster.

A scream formed in Josh's mouth, a silent scream that failed to come. He knew that Savage was unarmed, that the man wore no sidearm.

The cowhand never completed the draw. Savage moved. He reached out with his left hand smashing the whiskey bottle against the bar. The light from the hanging lanterns danced off the ragged edges of the amber glass. And then the bottle seemed to disappear. Savage's massive right hand closed tightly around the cowpuncher's gun arm. Forcefully, he pulled the man to him, with no more effort than if he were lifting a rag doll.

There was a scream. Sudden, high-pitched, like an animal in great pain. The cowboy clutched at his gut and backed up, his pistol tumbling harmlessly to the floor. His tanned face blanched chalk white, and he stared open-mouthed at his belly. There was a growing circle of red on his shirt; bright red, just above his belt buckle. Both hands were at his belly now, the bright crimson flow oozing between his fingers. He was holding on to something; something round, smooth. Amber.

It was the bottle, the whiskey bottle Savage had smashed against the bar. The cowhand looked up at Savage, his mouth working, the words inaudible. Then he looked down at his stomach again, puzzled, his numb fingers pulling at the thing that tore at his guts. He fell, face forward, the sound of shattering glass muffled by his dead weight.

Jake Kincaid came through the door, pausing at the batwings. He eased them shut, noiselessly. Josh watched as his uncle drew his revolver. And then the lawman was across the room, the barrel of his pistol gleaming blue-grey under the pale light of the kerosene lanterns. Without warning, he struck Savage from behind, the barrel of the Remington arcing through the air and slashing into the man's skull just behind the right ear. Savage went down like a great tree struck by lightning.

Kincaid's eyes probed the room. There was the slick sound of metal against leather as he slid the pistol back into the holster. 'Someone get Harper,' he ordered. 'And then I want a couple of you to give me a hand with the garbage!' He jerked his thumb at the fallen bounty hunter.

White-faced, he turned on the boy, his arm pointing toward the door. 'You get your butt out of here and over to the jail,' he bellowed. '*Now*!!'

CHAPTER 6

They made the ride in utter silence, Jake Kincaid leading the boy's mare. It was late, well past midnight, the full moon lighting the rock-strewn road. Josh stared ahead, watching the reflection of the moon off the backs of the silver dollar-sized tarantulas that scurried across the roadway.

He had sat for over an hour in Jake's office, watching the silent comings and goings. Logan Belmont, the young man Jake used as a deputy when the need arose, the old man from the newspaper, old man Berrigan, the barber. Then, finally, Doc Harper, and with him, Clara Altman. It was all like a dream to Josh; a bad dream, and he wished himself awake and sober.

Jake slowed his bay gelding, dropping back beside the boy. 'I should have kicked your ass all the way back to the ranch.' The man's nostrils were pinched, and his breath came in a thin white vapor on the cold black air. 'Drunk as a skunk, shacked up in the whorehouse like some . . .' He didn't finish, just shook his head. 'What the hell am I going to tell your pa?' he demanded flatly.

Josh dropped his head. Not with any great sense of shame. He was too sick to worry about his pa, the whiskey tearing at his belly as it burned its way up his windpipe. He reached out, grabbing his uncle's arm. 'I think I'm going to be sick. . . .'

Jake swore. He pulled both horses to a jolting stop, feeling no sympathy for the boy. Dismounting, he went to the sorrel and grabbed the kid by his belt and collar, pulling him to the ground. None too gently, he shoved him in the direction of a pile of rocks.

Josh vomited. He stood there, his head pressed against the air-cooled sandstone boulders, his body torn by the dry heaves. There was the sour taste of bile at the back of his throat and on his tongue. He shook his head, trying to clear the cobwebs, sucking in deep lungfuls of the cold, night air.

Jake led him back to his horse. 'Serve you right if I tied you across her like a sack of grain.'

The kid spun away and mounted under his own steam. 'Sure,' he retorted. 'You could hit me from behind! Just like you hit Savage!'

The lawman climbed aboard his gelding. 'I gave Savage as much of a chance as he gave that kid,' he said scornfully.

'Mr Savage was facing that cowboy!' Josh swung his face toward his uncle, his eyes bright, accusatory. Jake returned the stare, his gaze unwavering, boring into the boy. He said nothing; offered no argument. Unable to meet the man's silent scrutiny, Josh dropped his eyes, his voice lowering. 'The cowboy,' he started, 'Doc Harper—'

'—Couldn't do a goddamn thing,' Jake finished, his voice harsh. He stared across at the boy again, wondering at his stupidity. 'What the hell did you expect, Josh, with three inches of glass shoved into his gut?' Jake didn't wait for an answer. Spiteful, he kneed the gelding and moved out at a brisk trot.

The boy was unable to stop the shudder that coursed through his body. He kept remembering the way the man had clawed at his belly; the way he looked as his life's blood drained from him and pooled on the floor at his feet. The wave of nausea swept him again, made worse by the mare's gait as she took the bit in her teeth and followed after Jake's gelding.

J.T. was on the porch when they rode into the yard. He

stepped down from the porch, appraising first his brother, and then his son. He half-turned, and called over his shoulder. 'Will!'

Together, the two men unloaded the boy and led him up the stairs, J.T. on one side, Jake on the other. Will held the screen door open, standing aside as they carried Josh through the door, his jaw dropping as he stared in awe at his baby brother. 'Drunk,' he murmured. And then, louder, 'Pa . . . he's *drunk*!'

It was true. In spite of the sickness, in spite of the long ride in the crisp air, Josh was still drunk. The two men supported his full weight; held him upright, and (it seemed to the boy) kept him from floating away. 'Tend to the horses, Will,' J.T. ordered. He flashed a silent rebuke at his eldest son's hesitation, and then swung his eyes to his wife.

Sarah Kincaid's expression matched her husband's. Her arms were folded tightly across her chest, a frown pulling at the corners of her mouth. 'Coffee,' she said. She sighed, shaking her head in angry disappointment, and went to the stove.

They guided Josh to the table, easing him into a chair. He hugged the table top with both arms, his throbbing head dropping into the black comfort of his shirt sleeves. Every sound in the room seemed magnified. The metal clang of the poker as his mother stirred up the banked coals; the flat clatter as she dropped the lid in place over the grate. Then she was at the sink, pumping the water with a strange energy, and the whole house seemed to reverberate with the scream and screech of the pump handle. The water that poured into the speckled enamel pot seemed to be waterfalling from some too-near mountain stream. There was more to come. From the far bedroom, the baby began to screech, and Josh lifted his palms to his ears. He felt as though the top of his head was going to explode.

Vindictive, his father slammed a mug of coffee on the table. 'Drink it,' he ordered. 'All of it.'

Josh tried. Somewhere between his tongue and his gullet, the coffee stopped, dammed by a sudden convulsion far back in his throat. He tried to stand, knocking the chair over, and ran, staggering, toward the door.

They could hear the sound of his retching – J.T., Sarah and Jake. They stood in a tight knot around the table, silent. Will came through the door, easing the screen shut, his eyes on his parents. 'God, Pa . . .' he breathed. He turned, watching as Josh stumbled back into the room. The boy stood there for a time, his eyes trying to focus, both hands clutching the door frame. Suddenly, his knees buckled, and he began to slip, the rough wooden jamb slivering his palms as he collapsed like a wet rag on to the kitchen floor.

They took turns. Sarah and Will first, and then J.T. and Jake, pouring coffee into the boy and keeping him on his feet. The walking and the hot coffee worked as an effective purgative, cleansing the liquor from the boy's stomach, flushing his kidneys.

J.T. and Jake were returning from still another trip to the outhouse, the boy wedged between them. 'He must have soaked it up like a sponge, Jake,' J.T. grunted.

Jake nodded his head, grimacing as he shifted his shoulder under the boy's arm. 'Kerrigan said it started right after Savage left Doc's.' The barber had told him more, and he debated repeating what the man had said. *To hell with it*, he thought bitterly. Aloud, he said, 'Savage treated him to a roll in the hay with one of Fulton's sluts, then took him on a tour of the *cantinas* south of town.'

'God damn!' J.T. cursed. He rarely swore, and it made the words seem even more vulgar. He cast a look at his son, satisfied that the boy's brain was still whiskey dead. 'What about Savage?' he asked, the question coming in a near whisper.

'I've got him locked up.' He was quiet for a long time, working the thing over in his mind. They kept walking,

66

moving toward the house, dragging the boy between them. 'He killed a boy in Fulton's,' he said finally, lifting his head to gaze at the waning moon. 'That 'puncher from the Indian Territory. Laid his belly open with a broken bottle, just as cool as if he was some farmer cutting a shoat.' His voice lowered. 'Josh saw that, too.'

Both men were silent, the only sound the noise of their feet on the gravel path leading to the porch. And then Jake spoke again. 'Savage was going to leave,' he said. 'Harper told me that he was going on a one night tear, and then he was going to leave.'

J.T. stopped walking, aware that his wife was on the porch and was watching them. 'And now?' he asked.

Jake shrugged. 'I have to hold him, J.T.' There was real agony in the man's voice. 'There'll be an inquest . . .' His words faded. 'It's the law.' He said the final words as if he regretted having to say them.

'I tried to kill him, J.T.' Jake stared straight ahead. He felt the boy stir under his arm. 'I hit him with everything I had, and hoped to God that I had killed him.'

Josh had come around enough to be put to bed. J.T. and Will were with him in the bedroom, struggling to take off his boots. J.T. stood up, wiping the remnants of the boy's vomit from the back of his hand. 'I'll have to get a cloth, Will, and some water. You see if you can get him out of his shirt.'

'Yes, sir,' Will answered. He tugged at the left boot, dumping it on to the floor amid Josh's soiled pants.

'I can do it myself, Will.' Josh struggled to sit up, pushing his brother away. His head still ached, and there was a sore emptiness far down in his belly.

'You really did it up proud, Josh,' Will groused. He straightened, watching as his brother fumbled with his buttons.

'Yeah,' Josh retorted. 'I really did!' He said the words just as he meant them, a prideful arrogance in him. He grinned up at his older brother, waggling finger at him, inviting him closer. 'I got fucked, Will,' he whispered.

Will's face colored, and he straightened up. 'You watch your mouth, Josh,' he warned, his eyes darting to the bedroom door.

'No kidding, Will.' Josh untangled his rubbery arms from his shirt, his tone serious. 'Savage had this girl in his room.' He flopped back on the pillow, his arms folded behind his head. 'Leona,' he said, letting the name drift lazily across his tongue. 'She was . . .' He couldn't find the right words to describe the things he had felt; the things he had done. 'Yep, Will,' he bragged. 'I got fucked.'

Will's face turned a deeper shade of red. He had visions of their mother coming through the door. 'Shut up, Josh. *Just shut up!*' He picked up the pillow from his bed and heaved it across his brother's head.

Josh grabbed the pillow and hugged it, stroking it as if it were alive. He grinned up at his brother and began to make loud kissing noises. 'You should have been there, Will,' he whispered, sitting up. This time, it didn't seem as if his stomach was interested in mating with his brain. 'She took off *all* her clothes.' His tone was secretive, and he was talking rapidly. The pillow was still on his lap, and he hugged it tighter. 'She had the nicest set of tits. . . .' *God, how he loved that word; the things it conjured up in his mind, his groin.* 'She let me kiss them,' he shuddered.

Will was having a hard time holding his temper. He had a steady girl, in Sonoita; the kind you make promises to; promises that you kept. He had never bedded her – she wasn't that kind – and there were times, so many times. . . . He shook the thoughts from his mind, feeling himself becoming aroused. 'I've got to go outside,' he said hoarsely, 'to the jake.'

Josh laughed, aloud. 'Sure,' he said. He knew all about Will's girl; what she would and wouldn't do. About all the time Will spent in the outhouse or behind the barn when he was thinking about her. 'It's better with a whore, Will,' he observed sagely. 'Lots better!' He grinned up at his brother, refusing to let go, needling him.

Will turned on the boy. He raised a hand, pausing, and the shook a stern finger at him. 'You think you're real smart,' he said quietly. He returned the other's smile. 'What if she had some' – he pause was intentional – 'some *disease?*' he asked, feeling smug. 'What if she gave you a good dose of the itch?' He bit his lower lip, reading the worry that touched Josh's face and wrinkled his smooth brow. His upraised finger moved slowly down until he was pointing at his brother's crotch. 'It'll turn black,' he said ominously, curbing his need to laugh. 'Swear to God, Josh,' he declared. 'It'll dry up, turn black, and fall off.' He kept on. 'You know what the preacher says about those saloon women; what they can do to a man.' Remorseful, he shook his head. 'It could be bad; real bad. . . .'

Josh was worried. Wide-eyed he sat on the edge of the bed, his face white. 'Will. . . ?'

J.T. was at the door. He had heard the exchange between his sons, and suppressed a grin. Straight-faced, he entered the room, and crossed to the bed. He sat down next to Josh, his movements slow, deliberate. He wrung out the piece of toweling, and wiped it across the boy's face.

'Did you hear, Pa?' Josh's voice came through the thick cloth, a desperation in him.

'Did I hear what, Josh?' J.T. asked innocently, continuing to mop the boy's face.

Josh held his father's hand away from his face and stared him straight in the eye. 'What Will said?' he asked. He averted his bloodshot eyes. 'What we both said?' he whispered miserably.

J.T. shared a covert wink with his eldest son. He didn't exactly approve of the older boy's scare tactics, but he didn't disapprove either. *Serves you right,* he thought ruefully, *raising hell like this, putting your mother through this kind of grief.* He purposely hesitated before answering, sloshing the face cloth up and down in the pan of cool water, wringing it out a second time. 'Well,' he said finally, 'your brother may have gone a little bit too far . . .' He paused, swiping the cloth across the boy's face and neck a final time. His thumb rested just below the boy's right eye, and he pulled at the bottom lid, his face grim as he moved nose to nose for a closer look. 'Of course, I have heard of a man going blind. . . .' He shook his head, concerned.

'Blind?' Josh echoed weakly.

J.T. stood up, nodding. 'Blind,' he repeated. He picked up the basin, and stood up. The clock in the hallway chimed, and all three Kincaids counted as it tolled the hour. *One in the morning,* J.T. noted mentally, cursing the passage of time. He turned to his sons. 'You've got about four hours of sleep before the sun comes up,' he reckoned.

Subdued, Josh nodded his head. He felt miserable. His gut still ached, and his head was sore. *And his eyes . . .* He rubbed them, staring hard at the floor. They didn't seem to work like they should, and there was a soreness in them. 'Pa?'

'Your father is going to bed.' Sarah Kincaid had entered the bedroom. She had a clean nightshirt across her arm, and she held it out to her youngest son. 'How is he, J.T.?' She asked the question as if Josh was unable to answer.

J.T. swung his eyes toward his youngest son, the worry on the boy's face an inspiration. He was going to have a long day tomorrow, and he had the boy to thank for that. 'He seems better,' he said. He reached out, his hand lingering on the woman's cheeks. 'I'm a bit worried about his eyes, though,' he lied. He knew from the sudden spark in the woman's eyes that she understood.

Will stifled a loud guffaw, turning it into a cough. He edged by his parents, toward the hall. 'I have to go outside, Ma,' his tone and moves urgent. He excused himself and bolted for the door.

Sarah Kincaid crossed the floor quickly, her flannel gown sweeping the dust before her as she moved. She lifted her son's head, her eyes narrowing as she searched his pale face. 'You're right, J.T.,' she said, nodding her head solemnly. 'They look terrible, just terrible.' Considering the whiskey-induced redness, it wasn't much of a lie.

Josh turned toward his father. 'Pa?'

Grimly, Kincaid shook his head. 'Too late now,' he said. He heaved a sigh, rolling his shoulders. 'In the morning,' he breathed. 'We'll just have to see how he is in the morning.' He looped an arm around his wife's shoulder, patting her on the arm as she led him from the room.

Will came back from the outhouse. He had barely escaped without breaking into hysterical laughter. Just the thought brought a smile.

'You look fit for someone who's been up half the night,' Jake Kincaid greeted his nephew, finishing his last cup of coffee.

Will grinned across at the man. 'Pa told Josh he could go blind. . . .'

'Go to bed, Will,' Jake ordered. He tempered the order with a wide grin, finding it hard to keep from laughing, and waved the boy away.

The lantern was on in the bedroom when Will entered the room. Josh was hunkered down beside the table, laboring over the fine print on a picture that decorated their wall. Will joined him, easing the door shut. 'Pa said to go to bed, Josh,' he reminded.

Josh seemed not to hear. He pointed to the corner of the lithograph. 'I can't read it, Will,' he whispered.

Will turned his back on the boy, and began to undress. 'Well, you know what Pa said, Josh.' He tried his best to sound remorseful. Carefully, he hung his pants over the foot of the bed. *No sense telling Josh that the print on the picture was too faded to read in anything but full daylight*, he mused, vengeful. Turning back to his brother, he picked up the battered alarm clock from the table between their beds. He wound the thing, grimacing as he thought of the few hours' sleep ahead of him.

There was a full moon. Even with the lantern off, the room would be bathed in light. Will hated that. It was hard enough to sleep when the moon was still behind the trees beyond the house, but now, like this, with the full moon streaming through the multi-paned glass. . . . He shook his head. And then he grinned, biting his bottom lip. Studiously, he manipulated the hands on the alarm clock, pulling the trigger. 'Bed, Josh,' he reminded.

Repentant – worried – Josh nodded. He cupped his hand and blew out the lantern. He was tired, too tired to resent Will's bossing, and too worried about his sore eyes to care. Sleep, he thought. His ma always said that sleep was the real healer; sleep and God. Somehow, he wasn't sure that God would be listening to any of his entreaties, at least not tonight, but there was still the healing hand of sleep. He crept into bed, welcoming the clean smell of the sheets. ' 'Night, Will,' he said.

' 'Night, Josh.' Will lay down, the bedsprings creaking as he settled on to the bed. He lay there, his hands behind his head. He wasn't done with Josh, not by any means. His brother was getting to be a real pain in the tail end. The calf. Savage. And now all this trouble in town. *No, siree, little brother. You're not getting away with it. Not this time.*

The clock on the bed stand ticked, the sound magnified by the stillness of the night air. Will could hear the scratching sound of mice in the eaves, and the gentle creaking of the roof joists. A night bird landed on the shingles, scrabbling for a firm perch, and then it was quiet again.

Except for the even rise and fall of Josh's heavy breathing. He was on his back, snoring, the wind rattling through his nose. Every time he exhaled, there was the sour stench of regurgitated whiskey. Will sat up and pivoted on the bed, clenching his teeth as he swung his legs over the side. He stood up, easing the mattress and springs from beneath him as he rose.

Silently, he tiptoed across the room, his longjohns a white, torsoless phantom under the bright moonlight as he moved across the floor. He went to the high oak dresser beside the door, bending down to open the bottom drawer. He winced as the drawer scraped wood against wood, his jaws tightening as he slid the drawer open wide. There was a noise behind him, the springs on Josh's bed singing as the boy's snoring ceased and he rolled over on his side. Will squatted in the shadows, holding his breath, relieved when the noisy snoring resumed.

He reached into the deep drawer, pulling out the heavy remnant of an old wool army blanket. It smelled of mothballs and flower sachet, and there were small wormholes in the thick weave when he held it up in the moonlight for inspection. Spreading it on the floor, he divided it in half, more mindful than ever of the ticking alarm clock. He worked rapidly, smoothing the blanket as he squared the corners. Satisfied, he picked it up, and marched stealthily across the room.

He stood on the edge of his bed, balancing himself as he put one foot on the small night stand. Stretching, he secured one corner of the blanket to the nail that protruded from the top of the window frame, pulling the cover taut as he lined up the other side. The nail in that corner was bent, and he struggled with it, holding the blanket in his teeth as he worked. And then it was secure.

Carefully, he stepped down on to the floor, unfolding the thick cover as he moved. The dark blanket totally blotted out the light from the outside, the long white path of moonlight that crossed the floor shrinking as the young man finished covering the glass. He tucked in the coverlet, lifting up the night stand and placing it tight against the bottom of the shroud.

Only one small glimmer of light remained in the room. The pale glow from the lantern his mother had left burning in the hallway. It filtered beneath the door, more brightly now with the absence of moonlight than it had been before. Will swore softly. He started across the floor, stumbling when his feet tangled in Josh's discarded pants. Fine he thought, scooting them across the floor with his toe. He jammed the trousers across the bottom of the door, pushing them snug against the frame.

The room was completely dark now; darker than it had ever been in all the years Will could remember. Pitch black, the way it was when you stick your head under your blankets during a bad summer storm. Satisfied, the youth felt his way back to his bed. He lay down, not bothering to pull back the covers, and waited.

He had set the alarm to go off at two-thirty, just slightly more than an hour after he and Josh had gone to bed. Not that Josh would ever know the difference. He was sleeping the sleep of the dead. And when he woke up. . . . Will pulled his pillow around his head, stifling the laugh.

The alarm went off. Will had placed the clock close to Josh's bed, right beside his head. It rang loudly, screaming its brassy rattle into the darkness. Will lay still, waiting.

Instinctively, Josh bolted upright, responding to the alarm's call. He heard Will fumbling for the clock; could hear the *click* as his brother shut off the mechanism. And then there was silence; total and complete silence.

'*Pa*!' Josh screamed the word at the top of his lungs. The bed creaked, the springs singing as the boy untangled himself from his blankets. 'I can't see. *I can't see. . .* !'

There was a noise in the hallway, the sound of bare feet on the wooden floor. Will sat up, his fingers on the blanket at the window. Josh was still sniffling, still yelling for his father.

Kincaid opened the door, and – just as he did – Will jerked the blanket from the window. He stuffed it behind the small table and sat up, rubbing his eyes as he stared at the doorway. 'Pa?'

J.T. entered the room, swearing when he stubbed his toe. He crossed the floor to his son's bed. 'Josh,' he said, striking a match. He lifted the globe on the bedside lamp.

'Pa. . . ?' Josh stared up at the lantern. At the bright moon that stared at him from beyond the window. At the softer yellow glow from the hallway. He shook his head, confused. 'I couldn't see, Pa,' he said. 'The alarm went off, and I. . . .'

Kincaid picked up the clock. The damned thing hadn't even been set, he fumed, fingering the alarm trigger. 'It was a nightmare, Josh,' he said. He patted the boy's stomach. 'It's the whiskey. It'll do it every time. . . .' He straightened, pressing his clenched fist into the ache at the small of his back.

Josh exchanged a heated look with Will, his eyes narrowing when he saw the smug grin on his older brother's face. 'It was Will, Pa.' He pointed an accusing finger. 'He. . . .'

J.T. was having none of it. 'It was a *dream*,' he repeated. He yawned, tired. Impatient. 'Go to bed, Josh,' he ordered. He lifted the glass on the bedside lantern and blew out the flame, and then headed for the hallway.

Will held his peace until his father left the room, muffling the laughter with his blanket. He rolled over, staring at his brother. 'Josh,' he called softly.

'What?' Josh answered, his back to the other.

Will pulled the blanket from where it lay hidden and tossed it, his aim perfect. 'Now you see, now you don't.' he laughed.

Josh bolted upright again, a queasy feeling in his belly. 'Goddamn you, Will,' he breathed, untangling himself. He yanked the blanket off his head and tossed it across the room. '*God damn you!*' he yelled.

Carrie began to wail, her voice filtering through the walls. 'Joshua!' Kincaid's voice roared from the front bedroom; angry, tired.

Will turned over on his side, his back to his brother. *We're even, little brother,* he thought. *For the calf, and for all the chores I had to do when you were busy with your Mr Savage. Yep. All even.*

CHAPTER 7

Morning came with a white fire that burned through the window and scorched the boy's face. The heat and the light penetrated his closed eyelids and burned a bright red at the depths of his eyeballs. Josh shifted in the bed and felt his empty stomach roll, a sour ache at his throat and ears.

Smells drifted to him from the kitchen. Coffee, the sweet odor of apples and brown sugar. He could hear the sound of garbled voices, and then the high muffled laughter of the baby. He grinned, and found that even that simple task hurt. He didn't care. Carrie had a distinctive, early morning laugh. Wide awake, as if someone had whispered a particularly dirty story in her ear and she had understood.

Josh reached down, fishing for his jeans. He found the blanket first, the blanket Will had plagued him with the night before, and the anger burned in him again. He wiped his fist across his nose, his eyes lingering on the empty bed across from him. Made, of course. Good old Will never left the room without making his bed. *Piss on you, Will,* he swore.

Cautiously, he stood up. His head still ached and, as he worked the buttons on his clean shirt, he was aware that his fingers were numb; asleep. He stamped into his boots, his ankles wobbly.

His mother was in the kitchen, her sleeves rolled up as she gave Carrie her morning bath in the deep sink. She lifted a disapproving eyebrow as her son entered the room. 'You'll have to wait for your breakfast, Joshua.'

The boy cringed inside. *Joshua.* It was always Joshua when he had done something wrong; had behaved in a way that made her cross. 'I'm not hungry, Ma,' he said truthfully. He had the feeling that he had left his stomach somewhere back in the bedroom.

The tall clock at the end of the hall was ticking, the heavy pendulum sweeping back and forth. There was a noise as the mechanism began a slow grind, the chimes preparing to sound, and the boy braced himself. The bell tolled the hour, and he counted each loud stroke. *Five . . . six . . . seven . . . eight.* He opened his eyes, the chimes still ringing somewhere deep inside his head. 'Where's Pa?' Even his own voice seemed unusually loud.

The woman lifted the little girl from the sink, enfolding her in a large square of soft toweling. She was rubbing at the child's blond curls when she turned to face her son. 'The stock auction, Joshua,' she answered. 'Your father and Will took that string of horses to the sale in Tucson.' There was a long silence and she saw the look of anguish and disappointment that swept the boy's pale face. The horse sale at Bosman's was an annual spring event; one that both boys looked forward to. Four days of town living; hotel beds, restaurants, the good-natured haggling of men in a man's world. 'I want you to get washed up, Joshua. And then you're to hitch up the buggy.' She finished drying the child, setting her on the table as she began dressing her. When the boy stood his ground, she swept him with a long, disparaging gaze. She knew the reason for his petulance. 'It was my decision, Joshua. I told your father that I didn't feel you deserved to go with him to Bosman's.' As far as the woman was concerned, there was no further reason to discuss that matter. 'The buggy,' she instructed, impatient. 'We're going to see Miss Altman.'

The boy's brow knotted, then smoothed. 'But it's Saturday,

Ma,' he argued.

'I know very well what day it is.' The woman had lost her remaining patience, but she was not shouting. Her words were soft; whisper soft. 'You are going to apologize to Miss Altman.' She held up her hand when the boy started to object, swinging her arm to point at the Beadle's dime novel and neatly folded paper sitting on the sideboard. 'Perhaps, if you are fortunate, she will allow you to go back to school Monday morning.'

Josh knew better than to argue with his mother when she was this determined. No one argued with Sarah when she got all quiet and spoke so softly. 'Uncle Jake,' Josh said bitterly, remembering now that Miss Altman had been in Jake's office the night before. 'She told.'

Sarah nodded her head. 'Yes. She told.' She finished dressing the baby, fastening the buttons on her shoes. 'The buggy, Joshua,' she ordered.

The buggy ride was punishment enough, as far as the boy was concerned. His stomach was still tender, and the morning sun still burned at his eyes. And his hat. For some reason, the hat seemed two sizes too small for his throbbing head.

They were standing together in the parlor of Miss Altman's small house, Josh feeling like a two-year-old. The woman had a long list of grievances, and she itemized every one, Sarah nodding her head at each bitter denouncement. When the long tirade finally ended, she turned to her son, tugging at his sleeves. 'Joshua,' she prompted, her voice firm.

Josh would have rather taken a beating. He made the apology, hat in hand, chewing at his bottom lip as he carefully chose each word. He kept looking past the woman, staring at the ornate clock on her mantel. The apology took an agonizing three and a half minutes. For the boy it was like three and a half hours.

He felt little release when they finally left the house,

tagging behind his mother as they headed toward the buggy. He helped her into her seat and then handed up the baby. Hesitating, he cleared his throat, his eyes turning briefly towards the jail. Jake's horse was not there; not at the hitch rail, and not in the small pen at the side of the building. 'I want to see Mr Savage,' he said quietly.

Sarah Kincaid looked down at her son. She could not believe what she was hearing. Weary, she shook her head. 'Get in the buggy, Josh.'

'Ma . . .' The boy was pleading a lost cause.

'Get into the buggy,' the woman repeated. When the boy hesitated, she continued, 'Your father and I,' she began quietly '. . . and your Uncle Jake . . . have decided that you have seen enough – more than enough – of your Mr Savage.

'You will not see him again.'

Josh's fingers closed around the smooth wood trim on the small surrey. 'He's my friend,' he said stubbornly.

The woman closed her eyes briefly, rubbing at the dull ache that was centered at her forehead. 'Men like Rance Savage don't have friends, Josh. They simply use people, just like he used you. To run his errands, to help him move.'

She reached out, her fingers closing around Josh's clenched fist where he held on to the buggy. 'Your uncle—'

'—Hit Mr Savage from behind!' Josh interrupted, his voice rising. 'He came up from behind, like some bushwhacker, and bashed him in the head!' He tore loose from his mother's grasp, and backed away from the buggy. 'He could have killed him, Ma! He tried to kill him!' He turned, fleeing across the street, closing his ears to the woman's repeated calls.

Savage lounged back against the damp adobe brick wall. There was a bandage around his head, set at a rakish angle above one eye, the gauze covering the top of his right ear.

'Mr Savage.' Josh entered the narrow passageway, out of breath, and went directly to the door of the man's cell. He

80

reached out, his hand hovering at the grille vork, then closing around the cold metal.

Savage remained on the narrow cot, lifting his hand in greeting. 'Far cry from the room above Fulton's,' he observed wryly.

Josh nodded his head mutely. 'I wanted to see how you were,' he said. He couldn't face the man, his eyes on the floor. 'Uncle Jake had no right,' he said fiercely. '*No right!*' Somehow, he felt responsible for his uncle's ruthless attack.

The man on the bed grinned, sensing the boy's uneasiness, the smile not quite reaching his dark eyes. 'That makes two,' he said cryptically, forming a *V* with the first two fingers of his right hand. He turned to face the boy fully, answering the question before it was asked. 'Kilkenny, boy. Your uncle and Jason Kilkenny. They both got me from behind.' He touched the pulsating knob above his ear. 'From behind,' he repeated softly.

Nervously, Josh turned, facing the door to the outer office. 'You need anything, Mr Savage?' he asked.

The gunman shoved himself away from the wall and stood up. He could feel an urgency in the boy, a growing dread. 'Your uncle?' he asked, nodding at the door.

Josh shook his head. 'My mother.' He stared up at the man, embarrassed. 'She ... they ... said I'm not to see you anymore.'

Savage nodded. He strode across the floor of the narrow cell, digging into his pockets. 'We had some good times, boy,' he said, nursing the kid's feeling of obligation. 'Guess we can be grateful for that . . .' His voice drifted off, and he crumpled the wrapper from his last cigar, tossing the paper into the far corner. He began searching his pocket for a match, cursing when he found none. He contented himself with chewing on the cheroot. 'That little girl treat you right?' he asked, meeting the boy's gaze.

Josh nodded, his mood glum. He was thinking of more

than the girl at Fulton's. He was thinking of the cards and the whiskey; the woman at the greaser *cantina*. 'Those men,' he began. 'The greasers. They could have killed me.'

Savage nodded his head in agreement. 'Most likely.' He chewed on the cigar a bit harder, moving it to the corner of his mouth. It bobbed up and down when he spoke. 'Sure could use a drink,' he said, tapping the bandage on his head. 'For the pain, boy,' he finished. He was milking the kid's guilt for its full worth.

Josh could hear voices in the outer room; his mother and Logan Belmont's. 'I'll be back, Mr Savage,' he promised, edging away from the cell. 'I promise I'll be back.' He turned, heading into the dark passageway that led to the rear door, a quick shaft of on-and-off sunlight marking his departure.

Belmont stuck his head through the doorway that separated the office from the cell block, and then withdrew. 'He's not here, Mrs Kincaid,' he said, his voice fading. Savage grinned at the empty doorway. His first instincts about the boy had been right. He was useful; very useful. And in the near future, with a little luck. . . . He smiled, and made his way back to the cot.

Josh waited until he saw his mother leave the jail, hiding in the noon shadows between Fulton's Saloon and the hardware store. He ducked out of sight as she passed by in the buggy, pressing himself flat against the rough clapboard siding. Home, he pleaded silently. *Just go home.* . . . She headed instead for the doctor's office.

Josh didn't enter the jailhouse from the front. He had been careful to leave the back door ajar, just enough so the inside latch failed to hook. Carefully, he sneaked through the opening, pausing to listen as he made his way down the passageway. 'Mr Savage,' he called softly.

The bounty hunter rose up from his bed, quietly crossing the small cage. He smiled at the bulge in the boy's shirt.

'Josh,' he greeted.

'Whiskey, Mr Savage,' Josh began unloading his burden, handing the booty through the bars. 'Some cigars, matches; a couple of boxes of ready-mades.' He dug into his pocket, displaying a handful of change, gold and silver. A sprinkling of Mexican pesos lay intermingled among the other coins. He shoved his open hand through the bars.

Savage shook his head, closing the boy's fist. 'That was your money, Josh. If anything, I owe you.'

Josh withdrew his hand, grateful. 'It was money that you gave me, Mr Savage,' he reminded.

'That's right,' Savage said. 'To keep. I gave it to you to keep, for all the help. A real man always pays his debts, no matter how small.' He went back to the cot, pulling the straw mat up against the wall to cushion his head. He uncorked the bottle and took a long drink. 'Josh?' He held out the bottle.

The boy shook his head, grinning as he patted his stomach. 'Think I had all of that I wanted last night, Mr Savage.' He stuffed the coins into his pocket and cast a furtive glance at the closed door to the outer office.

'He's gone,' Savage said. 'Went off to fetch the noon meal.' He lounged back against the wall, nursing the bottle. 'Thought maybe the whiskey would get you, the way you sucked it down. Like water,' he observed, shaking his head. He stared into the shadows at the boy, waving him closer to the bars. 'Some things, a man's got to learn for himself, Josh. How to treat a woman, how to hold your whiskey.' He winked at the boy. 'I think you've got the woman part down just fine, son; just fine. Now all you have to do is work on the whiskey part.' He laughed – with the boy, not at him.

Josh pressed his face to the bars. 'You never told me about Kilkenny, Mr Savage.' Without realizing it, he was staring at the man's extended limb. 'Not all of it.'

'Kilkenny,' Savage echoed. He took another long swallow of whiskey, his eyes on the far wall, his free hand massaging the rigid joint at his left knee. 'It was in '76,' he began. 'The centennial year for the grand old republic,' he lifted the bottle in a silent toast. 'Winchester Fire Arms came out with a special rifle that year. A commemorative, they called it. The Winchester Centennial.' His voice drifted off into nothingness for a time, and he made himself more comfortable against the makeshift pallet at his back. 'They had samples made up special; exhibited them at the Centennial Exposition in Philadelphia that summer.

'God,' he breathed, 'it was a fine piece. Like the standard '73,' he continued, 'only heavier, and a larger caliber. A .45-.75,' he intoned. 'More striking power and range than the .44-.40. Almost twice as much,' he said, his free hand working the rigid knee again.

'There was an old German, a brewery man from St Louis. He bought three of them, the *One of One Thousand* rifles. He sent one to Philadelphia, another to St Louis, and the third . . .' He drifted again as he reflected on some long-ago memory that had very suddenly become reality again, '. . . and the third,' he went on, 'was sent to San Francisco.'

Savage got to his feet, suddenly. He began pacing the confines of the small cell, his back to the boy, the stiff-legged limp more pronounced, as if the reminiscences had brought back the old pain and had reopened the old wound to expose the shattered bone. His words came with a hurried frenzy now, at one with his pacing, and he took a drink between each sentence. 'They held shooting matches in the three cities; elimination matches beginning the last week in May.

'The final match was to be held in San Francisco, on July 4th,' he said quietly, 'Independence Day. Winner takes all; an engraved Centennial, and five thousand in newly minted gold coin.'

Mesmerized, Josh listened to the man. He watched as Savage continued pacing, his forehead resting against the bars.

Savage went on, continuing the narrative, 'I'd won the match in St Louis, and I'd made the trip west with the shooter from Philadelphia.' His brow furrowed as he tried to remember the other man. 'Stockard, I think. Pinkerton man.' He took another long swallow, emptying the bottle, his face red. 'And the winner from San Francisco,' he breathed, 'a green kid out of Texas named Jason Kilkenny. We were all there, primed for the big day.' He was quiet again, thoughtful. When he spoke again, his voice was filled with a melancholy remembrance.

'He was good,' he said, more to himself than to the other. 'He had an old '66 Winchester carbine, .44 caliber rim-fire. I watched that kid for three days before the final; exposition shooting for the crowds. Every time he competed; cool as the wind blowing off a winter lake. Thirteen out of thirteen, every goddamn time he stepped up to the line.' The man took another pull on the bottle, realized it was empty, and then rolled his shoulder to ease the ache in his back and chest. He turned, facing the boy. 'It wasn't hard, losing to a kid that good,' he said, and somehow the words rang true. 'God only knows, he earned the gun, and the money.' There was reverence in his voice as he spoke of the Winchester.

Josh stared at Savage a long time. 'But the leg?' he asked.

Savage's mood and voice changed, a hardness marking his lined face 'That happened later,' he said. Teeth clenched, his fingers knotted around the neck of the bottle. 'There were men – some men – that took it bad, losing the rifle to some green kid.

'One of them took it in his head to go after Kilkenny, to buy the gun, or take it.' He shook his head. 'The boy needed the prize money,' he continued. 'I could understand him needing the five thousand, and I could understand that he would fight to keep it.

'He was waylaid, on his way home. Not for the money; just the rifle.' Savage was silent, staring out the barred window. He looked at the boy, a smile touching his lips as he saw the intensity in the smooth face. 'Kilkenny went crazy,' he said. 'Started a rampage that left men dead all across New Mexico and Texas.' He lifted his hands in a gesture of pure horror. 'I could appreciate a man killing for money; to keep his money from being stolen. But not for a rifle, some damned piece of metal. . . .' His voice drifted with his memories, and there was a brief pause before he began again.

'That's where I came into it again,' he confided. 'They put a bounty on him. Five thousand dollars that first year; twenty-five thousand before it was over,' the man-hunter breathed. 'More bounty than I'd ever heard for one man.' He shrugged. 'So I went after him.' He smiled the grim, sardonic smile Josh had seen that night in the bar, the night the cowboy died. 'Only thing, the kid got behind me. . . .' He tapped his stiff knee with the dead bottle. 'He got his last man, got the rifle back, and then he got me.'

Savage nodded at the gimpy leg, then limped across the cell to the door. He reached down, pulling up his pant leg, exposing the deformed limb, the torn and scarred flesh. 'That's what a .45-.75 rifle slug does to a man at close range.' He reached through the bars and grabbed Josh's hand pressing it into the jagged hollow just above his well-muscled calf. 'Blew the knee cap apart' – he heaved the empty whiskey bottle against the far wall, the glass shattering – 'just like that,' he finished.

Josh pulled away from the man's grasp, rubbing at his own wrist, his eyes still on the indentation in the man's knee. *The thing that used to be a knee.*

'And from behind,' Savage was saying. 'From behind!' He made no attempt to hide the bitterness. 'Your uncle and Jason Kilkenny! They'd make quite a pair!' He laughed, but there was no humor in the sound.

'Joshua.' The woman's voice came from behind them; soft, deprecating. There was a quiet rustling sound as she lifted the hem of her dress and stepped into the corridor.

The boy turned, facing the sound, his face draining of all color. 'Ma,' he said weakly.

Savage stopped his pacing. He turned and stepped closer to the door of the cell, his eyes filling with the image of the woman. 'Madam,' he greeted, bending slightly at the waist in a polite bow. He straightened, his gaze locked on the woman's face. It was easy to see where the boy had gotten his pale hair, his fair skin and blue eyes. The woman was striking, almost regal in her bearing.

'Mr Savage.' Sarah's salutation was cold, nothing more than a polite response to the man's greeting. She met the man's gaze directly, unwavering in her returned scrutiny.

'You have a fine boy,' the man began. He could feel the woman's dislike like a cold hand across his face.

'I think so, Mr Savage.' Sarah reached out to take her son's arm, her fingers closing on his shirt sleeve. 'And I intend to do everything within my power to see that he stays that way.' There was a quiet challenge in her voice, and a stubborn determination that only a fool would dismiss.

A she-wolf, Savage mused. His eyes narrowed as he appraised the woman a second time. *A damned she-wolf defending her cub.*

'Ma.' Josh studied his mother's face. He swung his gaze to Savage, and then immediately back to the woman. There was an electricity between the two adults, something tangible the boy did not recognize or understand. Clearly, Savage appreciated the woman; her looks, the way she carried herself. And Sarah . . . Josh looked at his mother. Surely she could see the desire in Savage's eyes. Josh studied her face, the pink flush on her cheeks. She not only saw, she seemed – to the boy – to enjoy what she was seeing. Josh felt betrayed; angry. Jealous. 'Ma!'

The woman shushed him, her fingers pressed against his lips. 'We're going home, Josh,' she said firmly. 'I'm taking you home!' She took his hand, much the same way she had the first time he had gone off to school, and led him from the passageway.

CHAPTER 8

Savage watched from the window of his cell. He could see the woman and the boy as the buggy headed down the street on the road leading out of town. The woman was bareheaded, the wind lifting stray strands of hair that had escaped the bun at her neck, the setting sun touching them and turning them the color of burnished gold. *She's a real looker,* he thought. *And strong,* he reckoned. He had seen the strength in her manner, the quiet defiance. *Strong and unafraid.* The kind of woman who would do a man proud, in the kitchen and in the bedroom.

He turned from the window, fumbling with the pack of rolled smokes. He bent his head to light the cigarette and felt a sudden, sharp pain behind his ear. Kincaid, he cursed. Reaching up, he touched the spot, massaging it with his fingers, letting the pain remind him of his debt to the lawman. It was a debt he intended to repay. *In full.*

He laughed, then, the sound filled with a sardonic self-recrimination. He had yet to see the man face to face. The Doc had never allowed Kincaid inside his sickroom, and then on his first night out . . . The lump behind his ear began to throb again. Kincaid had gotten him from behind, had laid open his head like some over-ripe melon, and dumped him into the filth of the barroom floor. *Like some drunk; some common, whorehouse drunk.*

There was a sound at the heavy door that separated the

cells from the front office; he stared at the opening, his eyes squinting as the bright light from the outer room flooded the dark passageway. A man stood outlined in the light for a brief time, and then stepped down into the narrow hallway. 'Chow,' the voice called.

Savage pressed his face to the grillework, unable to make out the man's features. 'Kincaid?' he asked softly.

He was answered with the sound of soft, almost boyish laughter. 'Hell, no.' The man reached up, touching a match to the wick of the globeless lantern that hung on the far wall, his face washed with the sudden rise of blue-white light. 'Belmont,' the man said. 'Logan Belmont.' He turned, tapping the deputy's badge that hung from his shirt pocket.

Savage nodded, his eyes measuring the younger man. He grinned, hopeful. *The kid couldn't be more than twenty; twenty-one at the most,* he thought. *And green,* he mused. Hoped. He stood at the door, his eyes on the tin plate the other was holding. 'You the cook, too?' he asked sarcastically.

Insulted, Belmont shook his head. 'Hell, no.' He pulled his revolver. 'You back up, old man,' he ordered, 'and then turn around and grab yourself a handful of bars at that window. And you stay that way until I tell you otherwise.'

Savage looked into the young man's eyes, and then into the black hole at the end of the revolver's long barrel. He nodded a grudging agreement and did as he was told, crossing the cell to the barred window. He wrapped his long fingers around the rusted iron bars. 'I take it Kincaid told you to watch yourself,' he said over his shoulder.

There was a scraping sound as the deputy unlocked the door and swung it partially open. 'That's right,' the deputy answered. 'Jake has been at this a hell of a lot longer than I have. I figure if I ever want his job full time, I'd best listen to what he tells me. *Everything* he tells me.' The door slammed shut. 'You can turn around now, Savage.'

The bounty hunter released his hold on the bars and went

90

to the door of the cage. He bent down, picking up the plate and spoon from the dirty floor. The spoon was army issue, gray-green with tarnish. He wiped it across the knee of his pants. 'Kincaid been around a long time?' he asked, backing up to his cot. He sat, resting the plate on his outstretched leg.

'Long enough,' Belmont answered. He grinned across at Savage. 'That's why you're here,' he pointed out, 'and he's out there.' He jerked his thumb at the door.

Savage nodded, chewing on a chunk of day-old bread. 'Can't help but admire a man who knows his job,' he said, swallowing the lie. He stared up at the young man, calling out to him again, 'You got any idea how long he plans on keeping me penned up?' He wiped at the runny gravy with the dry bread crust. 'That 'breed was wanted,' he declared.

The deputy hesitated at the door to the office. 'Says you,' he countered. *What the hell,* he thought. *Wasn't any harm in telling Savage what Jake was planning. The man sure in hell wasn't going anywhere any time soon.* 'Jake figures on keeping you here until the inquest, and until he's damn sure there ain't no paper on you; no lawman lookin' for you. He ain't plannin' on keepin' you around this town any longer than he has to' – the youth grinned – 'unless you cause him any more grief.

'Then I figure he might just have to find a place you can stay that's more permanent, maybe, like the county plot out behind the old cemetery.' The novice lawman laughed at his own humor.

Savage paused in his eating, unimpressed, and dislodged a stubborn shred of meat from between his front teeth. 'You figure he's that good?' he asked softly. He tapped the bandage at his ear. 'I mean, *facing* a man, you figure he's that good?'

Belmont snorted, angry that the gunman doubted his idol. 'Better'n you, old man. And a hell of a lot smarter. Like I said. He put you here.' The deputy touched his forehead in farewell and disappeared through the outer door.

Savage tossed his empty plate across the cell, cursing at the sharp pain in his head when the tin ware clattered against the dry adobe and then bounced, wobbling, on the packed earthen floor. Kincaid would be using the wire, sending telegraphs all across the Territory, and east to New Mexico.

Texas.

One way or the other, he had to get out. And soon; very soon.

They were sitting in the buggy, Sarah and Josh, the baby asleep in a large wicker basket in the back seat. The woman had pulled off the road, pausing to give the child a bottle of warm water and to dose her sore gums with paregoric. She turned from the child, adjusting her blanket a final time, her eyes on her son's profile. 'Do you plan on sulking all the way home, or are we going to talk?'

Josh stared straight ahead, his chin jutting out. 'I got nothing to say, Ma,' he said, his tone the same as the woman's.

Sarah picked up the reins, clucking softly to the small mare. 'Fine, Joshua. Because I've got a great deal that I want to say.' She had done most of the talking when they left town, and it had been like trying to hold a conversation with a brick wall. 'I want you to listen, Josh. . . .'

'Goddammit, Ma! *I didn't do anything wrong*!' The boy turned his head, his fingers blue-white on the edge of the seat.

Sarah pulled the mare to a stop again, exhaling. 'When was the last time I washed your mouth out with soap, Joshua?' she asked. She was getting sick of the boy's foul mood and even fouler mouth.

Josh dropped his head, his jaws tight. He remembered only too well his last session at the kitchen sink; the taste of the naphtha-laced soap. *It was Will's fault,* he thought, *all Will's fault for making him lose his temper*. Stubborn, he lifted a noncommittal shoulder and shook his head, feigning ignorance.

92

'I'm ashamed of you, Josh.' The woman urged the mare on again, her eyes on the road. 'Ashamed of the way you've been behaving in school, and the things you've been doing after school.' She shook her head. 'Last night,' she continued, 'drunk, waking up the whole house with your whiskey nightmares. . . .'

'Will,' the boy murmured. He swung his head sideways, facing the woman. 'It was Will!' He had tried to explain before about the blanket and the clock.

'No,' Sarah said quietly, her left eyebrow arching when she saw the belligerence in her son's face. She silenced him with a single, withering glance. 'Will is not the one who took you into Fulton's. He's not the one who bought the whiskey, or encouraged you to drink it. And he is certainly not the one who—'

'*Piss on Will*!' the boy yelled. 'I mean it, Ma!'

Sarah grabbed her son's arm, her fingers digging into the soft flesh just above his wrist. 'That's enough, Joshua! More than enough.' She was whispering, her breasts rising and falling as she censured the boy. She lifted her hand away from his wrist, her arm shaking. *There's no point in losing your temper, Sarah*, she chided herself. *It's pointless, utterly pointless.* She composed herself, forcing a calm she did not feel. 'We'll settle this when we get home, Joshua.'

'Dammit, Ma. . . !'

Sarah slapped the reins across the mare's see-sawing rump, urging her to a ground-eating trot. 'One more word, Joshua, *just one more*, and I'm going to take you across my knees. . . .' She picked up the buggy whip then, cracking it smartly above the horse's ears, more for the boy's benefit than the mare's.

Josh clenched his teeth, his lips set as he stared straight ahead. She doesn't listen, he fumed. *She never listens!*

The boy was in the barn, unhitching the mare and still smarting from the tongue lashing his mother had given him and the long list of rules she had laid down. He unbuckled the harness, punching the mare's head when she wiped her sweat-foamed mouth on his sleeve. '*There will be no more trouble at school, Joshua; no more trouble after school. You will ride into town with Jake every morning, and come back with him at night.*' The boy's eyes smarted as he pulled the tack free and dumped it on to the floor of the barn. '*And you will stay away from Rance Savage, Joshua; far away.*'

He stabled the mare, purposely prolonging the chore. Then he left her, plopping down on a bale of hay, sulking. He'd lost his temper a third time during the ride home, cutting loose with a string of four letter words that brought a deep red color to his mother's cheeks.

She promised him a licking. She was up at the house now, waiting for him to come marching in like some two-year old, all sorry and full of regret. *Not hardly*, he thought. He pulled a long stem of alfalfa from the hemp-bound bale and began chewing on it, feeling sorry for himself. A baby. *She treats me like some goddamned baby!* Something poked him in his thigh, and he shifted on his perch, his right hand digging into his pocket.

It was the money. The change that Savage had given him, and the silver coins they had taken from the young whore's pimp in the alley. *Twenty dollars*, he marveled, counting. *Twenty dollars and a fistful of smaller coins.* He studied the cash, thinking of the bounty hunter.

Savage had treated him like a man, had let him find out for himself about people. About whiskey. Not like his ma, or his pa and Uncle Jake. Even Will. They were always telling him what to do, what not to do, and always chewing on him when things went wrong.

He stood up, surveying the interior of the barn. He knew that he should have curried the mare, and brushed her. Given her grain. That's what his Ma had told him to do, and what his father would have expected without telling. His eyes fell on the tangled pile of harness. *That too*, he thought. Jake was particular about the harness and the rest of the gear. *A place for everything, and everything in its place.* He aimed a boot at the mass of leather straps, and swore. *To hell with them*, he thought. *To hell with them all!*

He could see the lights from the kitchen window, the shadows against the curtains as his mother went about the business of preparing supper. From a distance, he heard the sound of hoofbeats, the soft measured tread of a horse trotting across the packed *caliche* in the rutted path that led down the hill to the house. Drawing back into the shadows, he watched as his uncle dismounted and tied up his horse at the hitch rail.

Josh turned back to the stalls. He would wait until Jake stabled the gelding before going up to the house. He wasn't going to listen to any more lectures, not tonight, and sure in hell not from his uncle. It was all Jake's fault anyway, that he was in trouble; Jake and his big lawman's mouth.

The boy began wandering about the barn, looking for a suitable place to hide from his uncle. He poked into the far corners away from the lantern's beam, remembering how when he was just a kid the unlit places had frightened him. He had never come into the barn after sunset then, when the shadows on the walls were giants and unnamed monsters in his child's mind. But now he welcomed the darkness, the mixed feeling of fear and curiosity that prickled at the pit of his belly as he followed the mysterious sounds.

He spied a packrat, the tiny animal scurrying along the stone foundation, weaving in and out beside the uneven rocks and small boulders that formed the far wall. Josh followed after him, stalking the creature among the hay bales and the old tools his father had discarded but never thrown away. He cursed as the rodent disappeared between two loose boards, his hunt interrupted. Then he laughed. The animal was on the other side of the wall, in the long narrow side room the family used for storage.

Josh went to the narrow doorway, taking the lantern from the peg on the frame. He struck a match against the rough siding and lifted the globe, adjusting the wick until the soft light spread into the dark corners. Carefully, he swung open the door and stepped into the room. The packrat sat up on its haunches, its nose testing the air, the lantern's beam reflected in the brown-bead eyes. And then it was gone.

The boy pursued it again, wandering in and out among the boxes and crates, following the miniature roadway cut by the animal's tiny feet. Farther and farther back into the corner of the long, narrow room.

The trail led up to an old cluster of canvas tarps, winding under a dark, cave-like fold. 'Got you now, you little booger,' the boy whispered the words, elated. He picked up a corner of the tarp and threw it back, the smell of mold and decaying fabric filling his nostrils.

The dust of many years lifted, danced on the air, and settled back into the folds and creases of the heavy, stained cloth. Josh stood there, feeling victorious, his eyes on the packrat's exposed nest. He went down on one knee and began fingering the treasures the small miser had hoarded away. An old thimble, an assortment of buttons, a rusted hoof pick. Josh brushed away at the bits of bright cloth and paper that lined the nest, his eyes on the glitter of metal. His knife. *The damned little thief had taken his knife!* He picked up the redeemed prize, wiping the handle against his shirt sleeve, and stuffed it into his pocket.

Hoisting the lamp, he began to explore the hoard again, pausing when he saw the corner of an old trunk beneath the turned-back canvas. The packrat forgotten, he shoved the tarp completely aside and fingered the leather straps.

He had never seen the trunk before, not once in all the years of his prowling. But then, he had never trespassed this far into the interior of the storeroom before. He set the lamp at his knees, raising the wick even more, and began working the first strap, pulling it loose. The leather was dry and brittle beneath his fingers, stiff as he attempted to pry it away from he rusted metal tongue. Finally, he was able to work the strap through the tarnished buckle. He repeated the same chore with the second strap, and then turned his attention to the hasp.

The trunk was locked, a fact that served only to fuel the boy's curiosity. *It didn't make sense to lock an empty trunk*, he reasoned. He rose up on his knees and dug into the pocket of his trousers, pulling out the knife. Opening the larger blade, he went to work on the lock, forcing the edge between the pieces of grimy metal, sliding it along; pausing as it hung up. Stubbornly, he worked the blade up and down, his movements slow; steady.

C-ll-lick! He felt the vibration as the lock snapped beneath his fingers. Closing the blade, he put the knife away. With both hands, he lifted the heavy lid.

The trunk was packed to the top, the faint scent of cedar chips still lingering on the stacks of folded clothing. Trousers, old homespun shirts; moldering leather boots and leggings. He peeled away each layer, and it was like turning back the clock. A dark suit, an old derby hat. The fragile lace christening dress – yellow now – that the boy recognized from an old tintype on his mother's dresser. His older sister, the baby who had been born and had died before he and Will had come along. More darkening daguerreotypes, somber-faced people Josh did not recognize, and then another layer of old-time clothing. His fingers dug deeper toward the bottom of the large chest, then closed around something solid.

He pulled the thing up from the bottom, shoving aside the softness of more clothing and disintegrating paper. It was heavy; eight, maybe nine pounds, and long – a tight fit within the confines of the old chest. It was wrapped in oilcloth and bound with heavy twine at both ends. Josh pulled out his knife again, sawing at the string, freeing the stiff bindings. He grabbed an edge at each end of the package, and pulled.

The cloth unwound, much the same way he had seen his mother unwinding yard goods from the bolts of cloth in the mercantile. And then the hidden thing plunked down on to the piles of ancient clothing.

It was a rifle. Dumbly, Josh picked up the lantern that sat warm at his right knee. He held it high above the piece, a single finger of his left hand tracing the delicate curlicue engraving on the exposed metal. On top of the barrel, just to the front of the ejection port, in bold script – *One of One Thousand.* His finger moved to the rear stock, to the silver and gold oval that was mounted there, bright white and yellow against the dark walnut. There was a date inscribed at the bottom: *4 July, 1776,* and above that, a finely detailed etching of men in powdered wigs and short pants. Above the engraving, in the same delicate, old-fashioned writing, the words: *The Signing of the Declaration of Independence.* Josh picked up the gun, turning it end over end. There was a matching oval on the reverse side of the stock and he rubbed it with his fingers, reading the inscription aloud:

> *Presented this day of our Lord,*
> *4 July, 1876 to*
> *Jason Kilkenny*

The words tore at the boy; assaulting his brain. Jason Kilkenny. The ambusher who had shot Rance Savage; the man who had made him a cripple. The killer who had left Savage to die.

CHAPTER 9

Jake Kincaid stood at the sink, his shirt sleeves rolled up to his elbows. He wiped his hands, staring across the room to the screen door. Sarah was there, looking out into the darkening yard. 'What's wrong, Sarah?' he asked gently.

The woman's fingers were locked around the door handle. 'Josh,' she said finally. 'He's supposed to be tending the mare.'

Kincaid hung the toweling across the back of a chair. 'He's probably mooning around the barn, sulking.' The lawman helped himself to a cup of coffee. 'Clara said that he made a proper apology. Slow, like it was being dragged from him, but the right words in the right place.' He joined the woman, his hand on her shoulder. 'He's going to be all right, Sarah.'

The woman shook her head. She welcomed the man's touch and patted his hand. 'I worry about him, Jake.' She smiled, thinking about the boy's earlier rampage, feeling a bit guilty at her participation in the sham the night before. 'J.T. and Will had him convinced he was going to go blind,' she said, unable to stop the laughter. 'I even made a fuss over his eyes, and how bad they looked.' She faced her brother-in-law, not quite as ashamed as she felt she should be. 'They did look awful,' she said. 'Still do.' The laughter came again. 'It's just that he was so damned' – she threw up her hands – 'pleased with himself. Big lady's man,' she went on. 'Big time gambler.'

Kincaid rolled his shoulders. 'They all have to grow up

sometime, Sarah,' he said, blowing into his cup. He fought the grin. 'He did make an ass of himself, didn't he?'

The woman's mood changed then, abruptly. 'He ran away from me in town, Jake.' She stared out into the yard again, raking the screen with her fingernails. 'I found him at the jail, with Savage.' She pressed her head against the screen.

'I know.' Jake's belly had begun to rumble. He set down his mug. 'Belmont told me.' He cursed. 'Damn him!'

'It wasn't Logan's fault,' Sarah said quietly. 'Josh knew you were gone, and that Logan would be there only part of the time. He timed his visits to avoid Logan. I was just lucky enough to catch him.' She was quiet a moment, reflective. 'We had a terrible argument on the way home. He was swearing like a drunken trooper, and contradicting everything I said.' She stretched, pulling away from the door, the imprint of the screen etched into her forehead. She rubbed at the impression, trying to erase the lines. 'I told him I was going to spank him when we got home.'

Kincaid jammed his hands into his pockets, his shoulders bunched. 'Well, that explains why he's taking his sweet time coming in from the barn.' The lawman stared straight ahead, avoiding his sister-in-law's eyes. 'A boy Josh's age isn't going to break his neck to collect some whipping from his mama.' He smiled down at the woman, reading the anger that was threatening to erupt, hoping for peace. 'Look,' he started, 'we've all been on edge, ever since this thing with Savage started.' He still could not bring himself to talk rationally about the bounty man. 'And we've all been pretty hard on Josh.' He wanted desperately to ease the woman's mind, to relieve her worry. 'Growing pains,' he said, trying hard to sound uncon-cerned. 'Even J.T. says it will all pass.'

Sarah sensed the man's unspoken concern. 'J.T. isn't here,' she countered. 'He wouldn't have tolerated this; not for one minute.' She studied her brother-in-law for a time. There was too much pretense in the man, too obvious a need to convince her that nothing was wrong. 'I can't control Josh anymore, Jake. When he's here alone with me – when J.T. is gone – he won't listen. Not anymore.' She considered her own words. It was true. There was something about the physical presence of a man that made a difference with a boy, that held him in check. At least that's how it seemed with Josh.

Jake's mood matched the woman's. He nodded his head, grim. 'I'll go get him, Sarah,' he said finally. He pushed open the screen door.

Kincaid strode across the barnyard. He didn't believe one thing he had said to the woman about Josh and his growing pains; not one. In the past week, the kid had run hell bent for leather, breaking a half-dozen city ordinances, as well as several of the original Ten Commandments, and there was no indication he was slowing down.

Even J.T. was worried. It had taken all the persuasive powers Jake possessed to convince him to make the trip to Tucson. '*Savage is my problem, J.T.*,' he had pointed out. '*If you don't go, Sarah will think that Josh is in more trouble than he is. I can handle it*,' he had promised. Aloud he said, 'I can sure in hell try.'

Josh stood amid the clutter in the storeroom, silent, his face mottled a deep red. The anger – the rage – still tore at him. A voice called out to him then, from the darkness beyond the doorway, and he turned to face the sound.

It was Jake. The man stood at the door, one foot poised at the threshold. His dark eyes swept the boy, settling on the rifle that Josh still held clutched in his hands. There was no surprise in his face, no wonder as he beheld the weapon. Only a flicker of pained recognition. His jaws tensed suddenly, and then relaxed, tired lines forming at his eyes and mouth. 'Put it back, Josh,' he ordered softly. 'Put it back and get up to the house.'

The boy shook his head. 'You knew. You knew it was here!'

he accused, his voice quiet, shaking. 'You!' He thrust the rifle at the man. 'Just like at Fulton's!' His voice was still trembling, the anger coloring his cheeks a deeper shade of red. 'From behind!' he raged. '*You shot him from behind!*'

Jake Kincaid's brow knotted, his face contorted with a look of momentary confusion. Then he shook his head, finally understanding. *Savage had told the boy; the son-of-a-bitch had told the boy about the rifle, and about God only knows what else.* He stepped into the gloomy storeroom. 'Josh,' he began.

The boy threw the rifle to the ground. It thudded into the dirt between them, as insurmountable a barrier as a great stone wall. 'Jason Kilkenny!' Josh hissed the words, as if they were obscene, filthy.

Jake reached out, taking the boy's arm. He felt the kid tense against his grip. 'You listened to Savage,' he said. He pulled the boy to him. 'Now you're going to listen to me.'

'No!' The boy wrenched free. '*No!*' He stood there, clenching and unclenching his fists. 'Big lawman,' he said, contemptuously. 'Big man with a gun. . . .' He stared across at his uncle, hating him. *Savage was his friend. The man had saved his life, had saved him from the 'breed whore and her pimp. And once, long ago, Jake had nearly killed him.* 'I'm going to town,' Josh breathed. 'I'm going to stay there until Pa gets back.' He hurled the words at the man, spiteful. 'I'm going to tell Savage!' He bolted forward.

Kincaid's shoulder lifted as he flung out his arm. He shook his head. There was no reasoning with the boy; not now. Maybe never. He cursed a boy's need for heroes, and cursed Buntline and Beadle for creating the myths. 'You're not going to town, Josh,' he said softly. He saw the sudden defiance in the boy's eyes and stepped fully into his path, blocking the way. 'You're going to listen to me, and for once you're going to do as you're told. *Exactly* as you're told.' The kid bucked against his hold, struggling hard to pull away, shouting a string of profanities as he fought. Kincaid reached down, unbuckling his belt. He pulled the strap free, feeling it snake from around his waist. He doubled it over. 'You're going to listen, Josh. Dammit. *You're going to listen!*'

Kincaid shoved the boy into the kitchen, his hand wrapped in the bunched collar at the back of the kid's neck. 'Sarah. . . .'

The woman looked up from the stove, the pot of beef stew forgotten. 'Jake?' She stared into the man's face, lingering on the agony in his dark eyes.

'I whipped him, Sarah.' The man said the words as if they caused him great pain. 'He was going to leave. He was going to go to Savage.' His eyes narrowed and his voice lowered to a near whisper. 'He found the rifle,' he said. Just that, and nothing more.

The woman inhaled sharply, her hand going to her mouth. 'Oh, Jake,' she said softly, understanding now the anguish behind the man's brown eyes. She pulled herself erect, nodding her head, her pale face drawn. Determined, she turned to her son. 'Go to your room, Joshua.' Her words were harsh now, demanding, and there was no sympathy in them. 'Now,' she ordered. It wasn't simply an aggravating game anymore, an innocent matter of a boy playing at being a man.

'He whipped me!' Josh swung his arm, pointing a long finger at his uncle. 'Dammit, Ma! *He whipped me!*' He inhaled loudly through his nose, his lower lip trembling as he fought back the humiliation of his tears. It was as if the woman hadn't heard. 'Kilkenny,' he muttered, his chest heaving. 'He's Jason Kilkenny.' He swallowed, searching his mother's face for some hint of compassion. 'A killer, Ma! He's nothing but a back-shooting killer!'

Sarah Kincaid struck her son, hard, a single, open-handed slap that brought a renewed flood of tears. 'I told you to go to your room, Joshua,' she repeated.

Josh lifted his hand to his cheek. He fingered the welt that burned across his skin, staring open-mouthed at the woman.

She knew! She'd known all along. He blinked, his eyelids fluttering rapidly against the salty sting of his tears.

His mother had aligned herself with Jake. The boy silently corrected himself. *Not Jake. Jason Kilkenny. Killer; bushwhacker.* 'I hate you,' he rasped. He backed away from the pair, his eyes raking first one, and then the other. '*I hate you!*' He turned, and fled down the hallway.

Sarah waited until the boy had gone, wincing at the sound of the slamming door. She turned, facing her husband's brother. The torment was still there, lining his face, ageing him, intensified by the boy's bitter words. 'I'm sorry, Jake.' Her words drifted off into an empty silence, and she reached out, touching his arm. 'What will you do?' she asked quietly.

'I'm going to Tucson,' Kincaid answered, his eyes on the corridor that led to the boy's bedroom. He could still hear the sound of the kid's muffled sobbing. 'I'll find J.T., tell him what's happened. And then I'll send out over the wire, just like I figured before.' He was quiet a moment, working the thing over in his mind. 'Savage is on the run, Sarah.' He tapped his gut. 'I know it; I can feel it. Somewhere, someone has got to have a flyer on him. And then. . . .'

'But now. . . ?' The woman's fingers closed around the back of a chair, the veins in her hands standing out beneath her pale skin. She was genuinely concerned about the man. 'What about *now*?'

'He'll stay in jail,' the man answered. He reached down, his fingers lingering on the butt of his revolver. 'I should have killed him, Sarah. That night in the saloon.' Lifting his hand, he fingered the badge that hung heavy on his shirt pocket, hating it; hating even more what it represented. He turned slightly, staring out into the dark night, and wished for another opportunity.

There was a warmth on his neck, and he felt the woman's eyes on him. It was as if she could see inside his head, could read his thoughts; his fantasies about an attempted escape, and how it would end. He closed his eyes, and pushed the dark thought aside. 'Jail,' he repeated. 'For as long as it takes, Sarah; he'll stay in jail.' The promise came through clenched teeth. It was the best the man could do.

CHAPTER 10

Josh lay on his bed, sprawled on his belly, his rear end still smarting from the whipping. He could hear voices in the kitchen; the soft, compassionate sound of his mother, and the deeper, more intense voice of his uncle. Silently, he got up from his bed, his ear pressed to the door as he listened. Snatches of words came to him. *Savage, telegraph, Tucson.* He swore, wishing he could hear more.

And then he heard the sound of his uncle's horse, the animal's hoofs biting into the dirt and gravel as he was kicked into a run. North, away from the town road, in the direction of the rim trail above the Sweet and the highway that led to Tucson.

Josh waited, back on his bed, the rancor he felt burning in his throat, wetting his pillow as it mingled with his tears. He did hate them; both of them. His uncle, because of the whipping and the lies, and his mother, because she had sided with the man against him.

He heard her footsteps then, heard her stop at his door and quietly step into his room. He screwed his eyes shut, facing the wall as he pretended to sleep, and felt her hand on his forehead. 'Josh,' she breathed softly, a contrite sadness in the single word. She bent down, her lips touching his cheek, lingering. Still feigning sleep, he withdrew from her touch. The woman sighed and padded softly out of the room, closing the door behind her.

Josh lay on the bed until he was sure that she was asleep, the house settling into the late night quiet. He got up and dressed, pulling on an extra pair of socks. Then, picking up his boots, he tiptoed across the floor to the window. He moved the small table and eased the sash open, grimacing as the black silence magnified the scrape of wood and the thump of the lead sash weights. Carefully, he backed out of the window, his fingers clawing at the sill as he lowered himself to the ground. It was a short drop, two feet at the most, and he tumbled to his knees in the dirt.

Still carrying his boots, he sprinted across the yard to the barn, slipping through the door like a shadow. He leaned against the door, catching his breath, and then stomped his feet into his boots.

He bridled the sorrel mare, not taking the time to saddle her, leading her some distance from the barn before he mounted. Satisfied he was far enough from the house, he kicked her into a full run, hunkering down on her neck as he made the ride into town.

It was late when he approached the main street, the narrow crescent of a new moon midnight-high in the sky above him. Only an occasional light flickered from the windows, the steady yellow glow from the doorway of Fulton's saloon washing out into the street then dissipating. He pulled his mare to a stop, and slid off her wet back.

He went directly into the barroom, ignoring the curious looks of the local businessmen, crooking a finger at the owner. 'I need some things from Mr Savage's room,' he said, looking directly into the man's red-streaked eyes.

'Like what, boy?' the fat man asked, unimpressed.

'Just a clean change of clothes, his shaving things,' the boy lied. 'Another bottle.' He smiled up into the man's face, a benign, innocent smile. There was no response. It was as if Fulton hadn't heard him. The boy shrugged, turning as if to leave. 'He told me to pay you,' he said over his shoulder.

Fulton's eyebrows rose as he considered the boy's parting words. He reached out a fat fist, hauling the boy back. 'I hear your Uncle Jake plans on keepin' Savage locked up for some time. Word is, the bounty man might be as good as hanged.' He studied the boy's profile.

Josh stared at the big man's reflection in the smoke-smudged mirror. *Savage isn't going to hang, old man,* he told the jaded image silently. Aloud, he said, 'Maybe.' He turned, helping himself to a small shot of whiskey. 'But Uncle Jake isn't sure.' He toyed with the glass. 'Thing is, Mr Fulton, if Savage is wanted, and the marshal comes to take him,' he shrugged, 'he'll take Savage's stuff, and tell you to send a bill to the office in Tucson, maybe even Phoenix. And then you'll be lucky to get paid at all.' He let his words fade, allowing Fulton time to consider his reasoning.

The saloon-keeper rested against the bar, stroking the stubble on his double chin as he worked the kid's words over in his whiskey-fogged head. He'd dealt with the law before, the federal law, and he'd gotten burned. Months and months of waiting; stacks of forms. 'You know where Savage keeps his cash?'

Josh dug into his pocket and laid a five dollar gold piece on the bar. 'Yeah, I know.'

Palms itchy, Fulton picked up the coin. 'He owes me a week's rent,' he lied. 'Ten dollars.' He rolled the coin between his thumb and forefinger, 'More, if he wants a bottle.'

Josh nodded, suppressing a grin. 'You get me two bottles, Mr Fulton. That Kentucky liquor Mr Savage likes.' He knew that the uncut booze was in the back room, and that the man would have to fetch it. 'I'll get his things, and your money,' he promised.

Fulton pocketed the gold piece. 'All right, kid,' he nodded. 'But I ain't going to wait all night.' He fished into his pocket for the set of master keys and handed them to the boy. 'This one,' he said, singling out the proper one with a quickness that hinted of a prior covert use.

Josh took the key and headed toward the stairs. He mounted them by twos, heading directly for the room that Savage had rented. He unlocked the door, remembering the first time he had been there. The whiskey. The girl.

Hurriedly, he packed the man's saddle-bags. One suit of town clothes, the rest more fit for the trail. Then the LeMat, and a proper pair of boots. He went back to the chiffonier and pried loose the narrow trim from one corner, reaching inside for the leather pouch. He'd seen Savage hide the poke that first night, when he'd been sent to fetch the barber, and had said nothing. Loosening the strings, he took out two double eagles. A bonus for Fulton; enough gold to keep the man from asking too many questions. Then he left the room, careful to relock the door, just as if Savage were coming back.

Fulton was waiting at the bottom of the stairs. He held on to the two bottles as if he didn't want to let them go. 'Your uncle know you're here, boy?' he asked, his fingers still locked around the jugs. He watched as Josh crossed the floor and placed the room key on the bar.

'Sure,' Josh lied. He opened his hand and dropped a twenty dollar piece on the polished mahogany. 'He sent me,' he said. 'Told me to give this stuff to Belmont, then get my ass end home.' He let the second gold piece trickle through his fingers, watching the man's face.

'Humph,' Fulton grunted, his gaze on the gleam of the gold coins. 'Then you'd best do as he says,' he croaked. He shoved the bottles into the boy's hands and scooped up the cash.

Josh made his way back across the room, trying hard not to move too fast, relieved when the batwings finally fanned shut at his back. He went directly to the hitch rail, untying the mare and leading her across the street.

A soft, pale light showed dimly through the barred windows of the brick jailhouse, the night air reflecting a blue halo around the openings. Josh lead the sorrel into the alley, ground-hitching her, and tried the back door. A new padlock hung from a recently installed hasp, a heavy metal plate covering the screws.

Josh picked up the mare's reins, cautiously heading toward the front of the building. He avoided the boardwalk, staying in the dirt roadway until he was directly in front of the door. Carefully, he mounted the stairs leading to the walkway, pausing at the top step.

The boy pressed his ear against the door, holding his breath as he listened for the sounds of movement within. Biting his lower lip, he eased the door open, just wide enough to slip inside.

Belmont was asleep at the desk, his head buried in his arms. Josh squeezed through the door, padding softly across the floor on tiptoe, moving in cadence with the sound of the man's snoring. He went to the hook beside the door that led to the cells and deftly removed the single key. Stealing a final look at Belmont, he paused, forcing himself to breathe slower. His chest was pounding, and he could hear the sound of his heart in his own ears.

The calm came to him slowly, his chest rising and falling more evenly as the fear began to leave him. *It's going to work*, he told himself. *It's really going to work!* Elated, he moved through the heavy door and headed down the passageway leading to the cells. 'Mr Savage,' he called, whispering the man's name.

The big man stirred, his hand going to his hip as he rose from the cot, the fingers slowly drifting down his empty thigh. He squinted into the darkness and swung off the bed, limping stiffly over to the door. 'Josh?' There was surprise in his voice; surprise and disbelief.

The kid nodded. He lifted his hand, displaying the key. 'Belmont's asleep,' he murmured. He started to put the key in the lock and felt Savage's hand close suddenly and tightly around his wrist.

'Too much noise,' the man hissed. He returned to the bunk and picked up the bare down pillow that lay there. Quickly, he returned to the door, shoving the pillow's thick bulk through the grill work. Deftly, he covered both sides of the lock. 'Now,' he breathed, pressing the pillow over the boy's hands.

The door swung open just far enough for the man to slip through. Savage reached out a hand, ruffling the boy's hair. 'Thought I'd seen the last of you, after the way your mother showed up to fetch you home,' he said, keeping his voice soft.

'No.' The kid's voice was filled with a strange determination. 'I brought your things from Fulton's,' he volunteered. 'What I could, without him getting curious.' He pulled the saddle-bags from his shoulders and held them out to the man. 'The pistol's in here; that and the money bag,' he confided, tapping the side nearest the man. 'I had to pay Fulton. Forty for your rent, for him to keep his mouth shut, and. . . .' He thunked the bag nearest himself, grinning at the sound of leather against full glass.

Appreciative, Savage nodded his head, his fingers groping for the gunbelt.

'What the hell?' Belmont was in the doorway, rubbing the sleep from eyes. He reached up, fumbling for the lantern.

Savage pressed his hand against Josh's mouth and stepped back into the cell, pulling the door partially shut.

The deputy started into the hallway, his eyes slowly adjusting to the darkness. Josh faced the man, the saddle-bags still in his hands. 'I. . . .'

Belmont's face darkened, his eyes narrowing as he recognized the boy. 'Goddammit, Josh,' he swore, stepping down into the corridor. 'Jake was here this afternoon, raked my ass over the coals real good for lettin' you get in here this morning.' The deputy took a step forward. 'He said if I caught you here again, I was to kick your behind all the way down the hall and back again, and then toss you in a cell until your pa could fetch you home!' He reached out, grabbing the kid's collar, boxing his ears with his free hand. Josh struggled to pull away, covering his head with his arms as he retreated down the corridor.

'Sonny?' Savage called out to the deputy. His voice had a taunting quality, and Belmont heard; heard and responded.

The lawman gave Josh a shove and turned to face the cell. 'You got something to say, old man?' The sarcasm in his voice matched the other's.

'Why don't you try that with somebody man-sized?' Savage challenged. He raised his middle finger in an insulting gesture, and then waggled it at the younger man, beckoning him forward.

Belmont moved to the door of the cage, his fist knotted, the boy forgotten. 'You pompous son-of-a-bitch. . . .'

Savage moved. He put his full weight against the heavy grille, one foot resting on the bottom grid as he pushed forward with the other. He swung the steel door full open with vicious purpose. It caught Belmont head to toe, knocking him off his feet. Logan fell backwards, hard, using both hands to catch himself. He was vulnerable, as vulnerable as a tortoise on its back. The bounty hunter dropped down from the door into the corridor, and, balancing himself on his good leg, kicked out. His boot smashed hard into the man's face, and the deputy collapsed into a ball on the dirt floor. The sound of his breathing was unusually loud, as if he were trying to breathe under water.

Savage reached down, pulling Josh to his feet. 'He'll think twice about knocking you around again, boy,' he said. Together, they stepped over the downed man, and headed into the outer office. 'You think to bring my horse?'

Josh shook his head, running to keep up as the man pulled him along. 'No.' He watched as Savage reached up and dimmed the lantern beside the door leading into the street. 'We won't have any trouble getting him from the livery, Mr Savage.' He followed the man out on to the boardwalk, still whispering. 'Old man Wilson gets drunk on his ass every night and passes out in the back room.' The boy ducked under the hitch rail and pulled the mare's reins loose. 'We can double up until we get to the barn,' he offered, thinking of the man's crippled leg.

Savage nodded. He gave the kid a boost up, and then swung up behind. The mare gave a little buck at the big man's added weight, and then trotted obediently down the street.

They rode into the open entrance of the livery, Savage ducking his head as they went through the double doorway. He slid from the sorrel's back, his eyes searching the stalls for the black gelding.

'Back there,' Josh said. He slipped off the mare's back and trotted down the passageway between the rows of stalls. When he returned, he was leading the animal. 'Tack's in there,' he said, nodding his head toward a sagging door. Savage hobbled over to the room and shoved the door open. He struck a match, using it for light as he rooted among the shadows for his rig.

They worked together, saddling and bridling the big walking horse, an urgency in their movements. Savage stared across at the boy, wondering at his silence. 'You're going to be in trouble, boy. Big trouble. That deputy saw you. . . .' He reached under the gelding's belly for the cinch, lacing the latigo straps through the ring.

'I don't care,' the kid replied. He disappeared under the other side of the black as he untangled the straps on the rear rigging. 'I want to go with you, Mr Savage.'

The big man inhaled. He had expected as much, and

wanted none of it. 'No,' he said finally. 'I take you, your uncle will be on my tail from now 'til hell freezes over.'

The boy rose up from beneath the gelding's belly. 'You need me, Mr Savage.' He stood there, staring up at the man. 'I can help you.'

'Not any more, kid,' Savage retorted. He returned the boy's stare, quiet. The boy was wearing out his welcome, crowding his luck. Savage debated the problem, his eyes on the street as he pulled the cinch tight. There were people out there, too many people. And if the kid made a scene. . . . He changed his tactic, his voice filled with concern. 'It's a hard life, Josh. Damned hard.' He pulled the cinch tighter, testing it, then drew back, plunging his clenched fist into the animal's air-filled belly. The horse exhaled loudly, and Savage jerked the straps tight a final time. 'I'm sorry.' He wiped his hand across his mouth and reached out, placing his palm on the boy's shoulder. 'I can't take you.' Insidiously, his fingers began to creep up the kid's collarbone, inching toward his throat.

'Even if I can get you Jason Kilkenny?' Josh's words cut into the black silence. Cold; terse.

Savage's fingers slowed and he cocked his head, unsure of what he had just heard. 'What?' he asked, his voice flat.

'My uncle,' Josh said, remembering the whipping. The hate filled his chest, strangling him. 'He's Jason Kilkenny,' he declared, spitting the words.

Savage came out from behind the gelding. He held the boy, a hand on each shoulder. 'What the hell are you talking about?'

'I found the rifle,' Josh answered. He didn't pull away from the man, just stared up into his face. 'I found the rifle, and he whipped me.'

'The Winchester.' Savage's face darkened, a strange red fire behind the brown eyes.

Josh nodded. 'The one in one thousand,' he replied, his

voice emotionless. 'There was a silver and gold plate on the stock, on both sides. One with a drawing, and the other with the words. . . .' He stared past the gunman, remembering. ' "*Presented this day of our Lord, 4 July, 1876, to Jason Kilkenny*".'

Savage lifted his hands from the boy's shoulders and then put them back, his eyes on the kid's face. 'You said you found the rifle. Where?' His voice was soft, beguiling.

'In a trunk in the barn, with a bunch of his clothes, other things.' He could still feel the sharp bite of the man's belt across his buttocks. 'I found the rifle,' he repeated, 'and he whipped me.'

Savage was grinning; a malevolent, calculating grin. 'What does he look like?' he asked. Josh swallowed, not understanding. Savage saw the question forming on the boy's lips and shook his head, silencing him. 'I need to know, boy.' He massaged the kid's shoulders with his hands, gently, coaxing the answer. 'I've never seen this *Jake Kincaid*,' he said, reminding the boy. 'Doc kept him away from me. And that night at Fulton's.' He reached up with his right hand, fingering the still bandaged wound.

'He knew you,' Josh said, his mind returning to the first afternoon in Harper's office. *Let him die.* He understood now, why the man had said the words. 'He told Doc to let you die.'

Savage was growing impatient, and he tried hard not to let it show. He had waited a long time to find Kilkenny; had spent a lot of years looking. The irritation was in his voice and his abrupt manner. '*What does he look like?*' he demanded a second time.

Josh felt the man's fingers digging into his shoulders. 'Not so tall as you, but almost.' He reached up with his hand, measuring. 'About a foot taller than me,' he continued. 'Dark hair, sort of curly. And slender, real slender.'

'His hands,' Savage demanded. 'His hands and his skin.'

'Long fingers,' Josh said. 'Like yours. And he's dark, darker than me. Like he's been too long in the sun.'

Savage released the boy. He rubbed at the stiff joint on his left knee. 'Where is he?' he rasped.

'Tucson,' the kid answered.

The bounty hunter nodded. 'He's gone to use the telegraph,' he reasoned, still nodding his head. He reached out to the boy again, careful to keep his touch light. 'When does he figure on being back, Josh?' he asked softly.

'Monday,' the kid answered. 'Sometime Monday.'

Savage grinned. *Two days*, he thought. *Only have to hide out for two days.* 'I can't take you with me, Josh. Not tonight.' He shook his head when the boy started to protest and dug into his vest pocket. 'We'll need supplies, boy.' He felt the kid's collar. 'You'll need more clothes.' He read the worry in the kid's face and slipped a reassuring arm around his shoulder. 'It's going to be a while before they find Belmont,' he said soothingly. 'And it will take another day – maybe two – before Doc has him patched up where he can talk. By that time, you can get the things we'll need,' he cajoled, leading the gelding toward the open barn door. 'The cave, son,' he said. 'Old Three Toes' cave. You meet me there, day after tomorrow.' He grinned inwardly. He'd damned near strangled the kid only moments before, just to be rid of him, and now this. . . . Repentant, he gave the boy a quick squeeze, patting his shoulder. He knew from the boy's face that all was forgiven. 'For the supplies, Josh,' he said, pressing a new stack of coins into the kid's hand. 'For the things we'll need.'

His left leg rigid, Savage pulled himself into the saddle using only his arms and shoulders. He hesitated, reaching down to ruffle the kid's hair a final time. 'The rifle, Josh,' he whispered. 'You bring the rifle.'

116

CHAPTER 11

Josh was at the breakfast-table, picking at the plate of scrambled eggs his mother had placed before him. He grinned, thinking of his late night sojourn, his secret adventure and the money he had in his pants pocket; the money and the things it would buy. Before long, he would be with Savage, and the two of them would be forever gone.

'You have chores, Joshua,' his mother said. She reached out, touching his arm when he did not answer, her fingers tightening when he tried to pull away. 'Finish your breakfast. And then I want you to tend to your chores.'

The boy stabbed at his eggs, still feeling vindictive about the whipping, and still angry with the woman because of her betrayal. Her lies. 'Why didn't you or Pa ever tell me about Uncle Jake? About the rifle?'

Sarah Kincaid closed her eyes, tired, her fingers kneading the sore spot at her temples. The boy had been like this since rising. Needling, badgering; pushing her to the edge of her maternal patience and then quickly drawing back. 'I've heard all about that rifle I care to hear, Joshua.' She got up from the table and took her full plate to the sink, scraping the untouched food into the kettle she kept for scraps.

The boy was unrelenting, persistent. 'Savage says . . . *said* . . .' he corrected himself, 'that Jason Kilkenny was nothing but a back-shooting bushwhacker, a . . .'

The woman slammed the tin plate down into the cast-iron

117

sink, her back still to the boy. 'I don't give a damn what that man has said!' She whirled, facing her son, her cheeks white. 'You have a choice, Joshua. You can go do your chores, or you can spend the rest of the day locked in your room.' She raised her hand in warning when he started to protest. 'I mean it, Joshua.'

She did. The boy could tell from the way her voice had suddenly dropped whisper-quiet, her mouth turning downward in a stern, no-nonsense frown. He dropped his eyes, unable to match the woman's steady scrutiny, his fingers going to the place on his cheek where she had struck him the night before. It still hurt, or so it seemed. It had been a long time since his mother had done something as harsh as that. Oh, she yelled at him, scolded him – he was used to that – but to actually hit him. . . . She had changed, he decided. She meant what she said; everything she said.

His gaze shifted to the screen door and sun-filled yard just beyond. There would be no sneaking in and out of his window, not in broad daylight with his Ma standing guard. No longer hungry, he pushed his plate away. He hated the thought of the chores she had selected for him, the long list of piddling, niggardly chores. But he hated even more the suffocating thought of spending the entire day within the confines of his empty room. He wiped his mouth with the back of his hand. 'I'll do the chores, Ma,' he said finally, rising up from his chair. *But just today*, he thought smugly. Whistling, he headed for the door.

Sarah Kincaid stared after her son, surprised at his sudden change in temperament. He was heading toward the barn, still whistling, kicking a mummified horse-apple ahead of him, as if he hadn't a care in the world. The woman watched after him until he disappeared inside the barn.

The quick roll of boiling water overflowing and sizzling on the stove roused the woman from her ponderings. She grabbed the handle of the teakettle, forgetting the hot pad, and then bunched her apron around the handle. She hated doing the dishes, had always hated doing the dishes, and yet the chore was as inescapable as cooking a meal or mending a torn shirt.

Resigned, she filled the dishpan. If nothing else, the chore gave her time to think. About her husband. About Jake.

About her sons. She plunged her hands into the hot water and watched them turn beet red. The boys were so different. Will was . . . She stopped herself, dislodging the older boy from her thoughts with a sudden shake of her head. You promised, Sarah, she chided herself. *No more comparisons.* It was also inevitable that she still make them.

The boys *were* different. They were, of course, a gentle physical blending of both she and J.T. and all the generations that had gone before them. But sometimes – more often, in the past weeks – she had the feeling that Josh had inherited every weakness, every petty meanness that all his ancestors together could have possibly possessed.

She had tried hard to pinpoint the *when* and the *why* of the boy's belligerent nature. For a time, she had simply thought it had to do with the arrival of the baby. She had read that somewhere, in one of the ladies' magazines the women in her church group often shared, that a new baby could cause all sorts of disruption within an established family. And yet, once he had gotten over the initial surprise, Josh seemed genuinely fond of Carrie. Sometimes, it seemed as though Carrie was the only one he did care about.

He certainly didn't get along with Will. He blamed his brother for everything; his forgetfulness, his bad temper. Even his foul mouth. Sarah laughed then, suddenly. When Josh was small, he had even blamed Will for his wet bed!

The shrill sound of Josh's out of tune whistle reached the woman's ears just as she finished the last dish. She pushed aside the gingham curtain, watching the boy. He was in the barnyard, scattering feed for the chickens, playing a hopscotch game of tag with the multi-colored rooster. His laughter rose and fell with the warm breeze; good-natured, full of rich humor.

Sarah shook his head at the transformation, thinking of the boy's pugnacious mood when they were at breakfast. *Very good or very bad,* she discerned. There seemed to be no middle ground with Josh. Not anymore.

Rance Savage stood at the mouth of the cavern, facing the north-east, relishing the feel of the air and sun on his face and back. He'd had his share of jail time in the past – had learned to accept it as just one more unpleasant aspect of his chosen profession – but each time, his coming out was the same. A rebirth; a spiritual reawakening.

He thought of the previous night and the things that had occurred. The kid, first. Showing up like an answer to some unspoken prayer. And then the thing about Kilkenny. The gunman raked his long fingers through his hair. *Twenty years,* he mused. *For twenty years he had searched for the man, had followed one false lead after another, riding long trails that had led nowhere.* His left hand dropped to the stiff knee again, and he rubbed at the renewed pain. *Twenty years.* And then it had fallen right into his lap.

He eased down on to a rock at the mouth of the cave, pulling the LeMat from its holster. He studied the piece, his fingers caressing the barrel. *To the victor, the spoils,* he mused, a trophy taken from a downed prey. He balanced the piece in his palm, smiling. More civilized than the taking of an ear or a head, or a man's scalp. More practical. He couldn't remember the dead man's face – there were few that he did remember – but he did appreciate the man's choice of weapons and his creativity and genius in rigging the complex belt and swivel holster.

The LeMat was a fearful weapon. Savage, well-read by frontier standards, knew its history well: Dr Jean LeMat's personal contribution to the Cause, the Confederacy. Single action, designed for close quarter fighting; a nine-shot .40 caliber revolver with a central bore capable of discharging a 16 gauge buckshot charge. At close range, a man killer. Close enough, with a simple flick of the finger to switch the movable hammer to the 'shot' position, it could take down a horse. Savage stroked the barrel, the pistol resting on the thigh of his extended left leg.

Ten years ago, he had taken this weapon, this effective mutilator of bone and flesh, for one reason and one reason only: Jason Kilkenny. To kill the man. Slowly, one piece at a time.

His mother had put him to work in her garden. Josh was on his knees, straddling the rows of seedlings she had planted, pulling out the weeds that poked up from the brown soil. He wiped a dusty hand across his sweat-soaked brow. *Squaw's work*, he thought bitterly. He sat back on his heels, pulling his shirt away from his chest, fanning it in and out as he sought some relief from the sun. *It would be different when he was with Savage*, he vowed. Damned different.

There was a noise on the horizon, the distinctive roll of shod hoofs. The boy resumed his chore, dismissing the riders as passers-by. Cowhands, he assumed. Sunday morning stragglers returning from a Saturday night tear.

Then he heard the slow, *spur-r-rong* of the tightly coiled spring on the kitchen screen, and the soft footfall of his mother as she crossed the porch. She was down the steps and running across the yard, lifting the hem of her dress as she ran toward the road.

Josh turned, rising up on his knees, one hand shading his eyes. *It was Pa! Pa and Will!* He watched as the came into the yard. J.T. dismounted from his gelding as it still moved, measuring his stride with the animal's. He reached out, enfolding the woman in his arms, and lifted her off her feet, his lips pressed solidly on her mouth. They held each other for a long time.

Josh was on his feet, his chest tight. He watched as his older brother dismounted and led the two sweating horses into the barn. They were early – a full day early. Sullen, he watched as his parents came toward the house, arm in arm. They paused at the bottom of the stairs, the man's arm dropping to the woman's waist as he held her back. 'Josh,' he greeted softly. He stood there, studying the boy for a time, waiting for a returned greeting. It came, finally. Nothing verbal, just a curt nod.

Together, the man and woman went into the house, their voices hushed as they spoke. Josh leaned against the corner of the house, beneath the open kitchen window, listening intently to their quiet conversation; straining to hear.

'Your ears'll fall off, you make a habit out of that.'

Josh spun around, his face white. It was surprising just how much Will's voice had begun to sound like their pa's. 'Why don't you just kiss my ass?' he suggested.

Will's face mirrored his brother's. White; drawn. 'I told Pa about the thing with the blanket, Josh,' he began. 'He told me I was wrong, that I had no business taking things that far . . . so. . . .' He looked like he was in pain, and took a deep breath. 'So I'm telling you I'm sorry. For the blanket.' He kept his words quiet. 'You're getting to be a pain, Josh; a real pain.' He reached out, his hand resting heavy on his brother's shoulder. 'Uncle Jake was in Tucson last night, Josh,' he began. 'I don't know what he said to Pa, what they talked about, but I do know that Pa sold ten head of prime saddle stock at a big loss, just so we could get back here.'

Josh knocked his brother's hand away. 'Well, I know what they were talking about, big brother. They talked about Uncle Jake. About how he killed a string of men all across New Mexico and Texas, and got a price on his head! Twenty-five thousand dollars, Will. *Twenty . . . five . . . thousand . . . dollars!*'

He punctuated each word with a thump of his rigid forefinger against his brother's chest. Josh watched his brother's changing face, enjoying the pain he was inflicting. Next to their pa, Will thought the sun rose and set on Jake Kincaid's shoulders. 'They talked about how he back-shot Rance Savage—'

'That's a lie! *A goddamned lie!*' Will hissed. He shot a worried look at the open window above them. Neither boy was yelling; not out loud. They knew better, both of them well acquainted with their parents' views on fraternal feuding.

Josh kept pushing. With his words as well as his hands. 'The hell it is!' He was losing control again, his voice rising. 'Twenty-five thousand dollars,' he goaded. 'That was the bounty, and Savage was hired to take it!' He ducked as his brother threw a punch, dancing away. Fists clenched, he jabbed at his brother, with his hands as well as his words. 'Uncle . . . Jake . . . bush-whacked . . . him . . . Will. Shot . . . him . . . from . . . behind!' He rushed his brother, pummeling his chest with a flurry of blows. 'Snuck up on him, just like he did at Fulton's, and. . . .' He bobbed away.

'Damn you!' Will swung, charging the younger boy. This time he connected, his fist glancing off Josh's exposed chin. He knocked the boy off his feet and then moved in, reaching down to pull Josh up for more. Right fist upraised, he grabbed a handful of shirt, oblivious to the rain of feeble punches, the blood congested in his face.

'*Will!*' J.T.'s voice thundered from the porch. He stood there, his big hands wrapped around the gray railing, looking down at his sons like some brooding giant. His face was mottled, a deep purple.

Josh scrambled to his feet, raising a cloud of brown dust. 'He started it, Pa!' He put the fingers of his right hand to his bottom lip, tongue and forefinger meeting. There was blood; warm, salty.

The elder Kincaid remained unmoved by his son's declaration of innocence. He stood there, his hands kneading the painted railing as he fought his growing temper under control. The rage was still in his voice when he spoke. 'Get in the house,' he ordered, his voice deceptively soft. 'Both of you. We're going to talk.' Resolute, he turned his back on both youths and stomped back into the kitchen. The sound of his sons' footsteps echoed reluctantly behind him.

He was facing them when they came through the door. 'Sit down,' he commanded, nodding to the table. There was a loud scraping sound as both boys pulled out their chairs, the sound recurring, muted, when they sat down and slid them back into place. Kincaid remained on his feet, silent. He waited until his wife returned to the room, and then began. His voice was barely above a shallow whisper, mindful of the child who slept in the room at the end of the long hall. 'Your uncle rode to Tucson last night, Josh. He told me what happened; all of it. About your going to the jail to see Savage, about what happened after. . . .'

'About the whipping?' Josh was on his feet, his fists knotted at his sides. 'Did he tell you how he took his belt and licked me like I was some baby?'

Kincaid nodded his head. 'He told me, Josh,' he said quietly. He reached out his hand, forcing the boy back into the chair. 'Do you think that it would have been any different if I had been here?' he said harshly. He shook a finger at his son. 'I should have punished you that first night. Drunk or sober, I should have taken my belt and whipped you from here to Sunday!

'That was *my* mistake, Josh. I thought, with time, you'd come to your senses and realize you were wrong. About all the trouble; about Savage,' he finished. His voice was whisper-soft again, the disappointment deep in his eyes when he saw the continued defiance in his son's face.

Josh's head snapped up, and he straightened in the chair as if he were going to rise again. 'I'm not wrong,' he said stubbornly. 'Rance Savage is my friend! He treats me like I'm a

124

man! And he isn't any back-shooting, head-thumping sneak like Uncle Jake!' He turned facing his brother. 'Like Jason Kilkenny!'

There was a long silence in the room, the quiet so intense that the noise of mice scurrying in the rafters resounded like the padding of thousands of small feet. The soft drag of the pendulum on the tall clock at the end of the hall echoed throughout all the rooms, making its presence known as it stole away precious minutes and aged them all. Will raised his eyes to his father's face. The question formed on his lips, then faded unspoken. He'd read about Jason Kilkenny in the same books that had carried the stories of Savage and Earp. A long time ago. Only he had known the stories for what they were, fairy-tales and fantasies for boys; for men wishing to be boys. He returned his brother's heated surveillance with a look of compassion, his brow furrowing.

Josh saw the look on his brother's face and read it as one of total ignorance. He laughed; a coarse, humorless laugh. 'Tell him, Pa! Tell him about Jason Kilkenny. About the rifle!' He braced the man, his face scarlet. '*Tell him about Uncle Jake*,' he demanded. He jumped to his feet again, knocking his chair over as he stood up. '*Tell him!*'

'All right, Josh,' Kincaid agreed, a cold calm embracing him. Callously, he reached out and pulled the boy around the table, his hand knotted in the boy's collar. He drew his son to him, standing close to him; above him. 'We were in Texas,' he began. 'Those of us that were left. My mother – Jake – me. With a trunkful of Confederate money, *paper money*, that wasn't even good for chinking the holes in the walls of the house.

'My father had died in the War.' A grim smile touched Kincaid's face, pulling at one corner of his mouth. 'At least, that's what we heard. We never knew; not really. We just knew that he never came back.

'We had the land, and we worked it. A lone woman, two

125

half-grown boys. Fighting the Comanche, the carpetbaggers.'
He paused, the memories painful. 'Our neighbors.

'But in the end,' he continued, 'we had over two thousand
head of cattle ready to drive.' He smiled, everywhere but his
eyes, his gaze on the far wall. There was no humor, no joy, in
the expression, just a wry irony that touched the man's lips
and kindled a fire deep in his moist eyes. 'A bug,' he said cryptically, measuring some minute, infinitesimal unseen thing
between his thumb and forefinger. '*A goddamn bug. . . .*' He
was silent, someplace far from this room, his fingers probing
into his pockets. He did a thing that neither boy had ever see
him do before, he rolled a smoke, slowly, his hands seeming
to shake. He lit up and inhaled deeply, welcoming the seda-
tive bite of the nicotine, pulling it deep into his lungs. 'A tick,'
he said. His shoulders dropped, and he took another deep
drag on the cigarette. He was reliving it; every bitter, gut-shak-
ing mile. 'We headed north from San Antonio, up the
Western, consigning more cattle as we went. Until there were
three separate outfits and more than seven thousand head of
branded and maverick cows.' In his mind, he could still hear
the sound, the low bawling of the cows and the shuffling, dust-
raising drag of their feet. 'Good weather,' he said softly.
'Plenty of grass and water. Everything like it should be.' He
wiped the back of his hand across his mouth. 'Even the
Indians seemed to be working with us. . . .' His voice lowered
then, becoming a flat, quiet monotone. 'They began to drop,
like flies; ten, twenty cows at a time, two, maybe three times a
day. We tried to save what we could, dose the ones we were
able to keep on their feet.

'And then we got to the line, the Kansas line.' His hand
went to his mouth again, nervously smoothing his mustache.
'They met us there, Lazurus' – how long had it been since he
had thought of the old man? – 'Lazurus and his company of
regulators, and the crews that had come north and east ahead
of us. They were afraid of the cows we had left, afraid they

were carrying the fever.' He shook his head, puffing on the smoke. 'I don't know. Maybe they were.'

He lowered his head, facing his youngest son, his eyes burning into the boy. 'What I do know is that they held rifles on us while they made us dig trenches; pits. And then they drove our cattle into those holes, and they slaughtered them. Lines of men,' he said softly. 'Firing into the pits, reloading, cramming in more cattle, firing again and again.

'We lost fifty per cent of the herd to the fever, and stood by watching while the rest were driven into the holes and slaughtered.' Kincaid reached out, cupping his hand beneath Josh's chin. 'That's when we heard about the rifles,' he said. 'Jake and I. We were in Kansas City, both of us more than a fair hand with a rifle. We read about the competitions, the prizes.' He crushed out the smoldering stub of his cigarette and began building another. 'We sold our horses, our handguns. Anything we could, except for the clothes on our backs and our rifles. For train fare,' he breathed, remembering, 'and for fee money. And then,' he said, the words coming stronger, 'we flipped a coin. To see which one of us would go to St Louis, and which one would go to San Francisco.'

Josh exhaled, flashing a truculent, triumphant look at Will. 'Uncle Jake,' he hissed. 'Uncle Jake went to San Francisco.' There was an air of arrogant righteousness about him.

Kincaid bent his head, lighting the second cigarette. He blew out the match, the smoke a blue circle around his head. He reached out with his right hand, touching the boy's shoulder, his cigarette close to the kid's ear; warm. 'J.T., Josh,' he breathed, exhaling a thin stream of smoke as he spoke. 'Jason Thomas Kilkenny.

'I went to San Francisco. *I* won the rifle.'

The dead, cold silence was there again, filling the room. Josh backed away, his mouth open as he unpeeled his father's fingers from his shoulders. 'No,' he said. The empty silence hung between them, the boy refusing to believe. 'Pa.' He was

127

pleading now. 'You wouldn't have done that.' He was thinking of Savage, his throat burning. 'Not you, Pa,' he was shaking his head, the tears building. 'Not from behind, Pa. *Not from behind*!'

Kincaid nodded grimly. 'I should have killed him, Josh.' He reached out to the boy again, his hand clutching air as his son retreated from his touch. 'I should have killed him!' he repeated. He watched as the boy disappeared down the dark hallway.

CHAPTER 12

They were in the bedroom, father and son, an invisible barrier between them, the boy sitting straight-backed and unyielding on the edge of the bed. His fingers dug into the mattress, his bent knuckles blue-white. The elder Kincaid stood between the bed and door, afraid the boy would try to run again. 'I won the rifle,' he said, exploring his son's face, 'and the five thousand dollars.' The sad smile was there again. 'It was money to make a fresh start, to buy a new beginning. I was married to your mother then, and we had the baby. . . .' It surprised the man that it still pained him to think about a child he had held close only once. He cleared his throat, his chest heaving. 'I sent the prize money home, to your mother; five thousand and extra cash I'd made doing competitions for some high-toned hunt clubs. Jake—' He paused, remembering. 'Jake didn't make it to St Louis, but it didn't matter. By fall, we had another eight thousand dollars.

'Eight thousand dollars, and a prize Winchester.' He was quiet a moment, choosing his next words carefully, wanting the boy to understand. 'I figured I could use the rifle to make some more money, that I could give some shows along the way home.

' "*Come one, come all*",' he parroted, remembering the bally-hoo. ' "*Try your luck against the champion and the One in One Thousand*!!" It was a profitable sideline, Josh, shooting against

129

all-comers. Winning, building the stake money a little at a time.

'Hell. I was twenty-one years old and I had it all. The big money; the best rifle in the world. A wife waiting for me.' His voice faded again.

'I made it as far as New Mexico without any real trouble. The Winchester tucked under my knee, and another three thousand dollars in winnings stuck in my money belt.

'That's when they caught up with me. Cash Santree, Lucas Dunbar.' He listed their names slowly, his eyes cold, deadly; the old hatreds coming back. 'Simon Cantrell.' He stared into the gathering darkness at the corner of the room. 'Your mother was going to meet me in Socorro,' he said softly. 'Your mother, the baby, Uncle Jake and your grandmother. We were going to look for land; new land, somewhere away from Texas, from the fever.

'Santree and the others were on the same train, following my mother and Jake. They came for the rifle, not the money.' He said the words again, as if he still couldn't believe them. 'They just wanted the damn gun!

'I'd found a place, just south of Socorro. Good graze; water. A small adobe house and some outbuildings. . . .'

Josh was still on the bed, still rigid and unyielding. 'And Savage?' he demanded, his tone sarcastic, scathing.

Kincaid's tone was the same as the boy's when he answered. 'You're going to listen, Josh. *You're going to hear it all!*' His voice rose. '*You're going to shut up and listen to it all!*' He watched as the boy jammed his fists over his ears. Cursing, he crossed the room. He grabbed the boy's wrists and pulled his clenched fists away from his head. 'I hired a buggy,' he said, talking rapidly, 'to take your mother, grandmother and Jake to the ranch.' He was hunkered down in front of the kid now, struggling to hold the boy's hands away from his ears. 'The three men I told you about. They followed us, Josh. And when we got far enough out of town – far enough where no one could hear – they cut down on us. . . .'

The man's face was red; deep red, the blood rising under his skin as his heart pumped within his tight chest. 'It didn't make a damn to them that your mother and grandmother were with me, or the baby. They came down out of those hills like' – he searched for the word, unable to find one vile enough to convey his feelings – 'like rabid animals. Your Uncle Jake was the first to go down, a bullet in his back. Then your grandmother. And then your *mother*, Josh.' He felt the boy stop struggling and reached out, his thumb on the button of the boy's chin. 'She was holding the baby. . . .' He swung his eyes away from his son, swallowing hard. 'It was such a little hole,' he said, the pain in his chest making it difficult to talk. 'Smaller than the tip of your little finger' – he reached around the boy's shoulder and touched a place on Josh's back just to the left of his right shoulder blade – 'where it went in.' He thumped his index finger against the boy's skin, and closed his eyes, seeing again the look on his wife's face when she lifted the shattered child away from her own torn shoulder. 'The baby, Josh.' He opened his eyes and stared into his son's eyes. 'Dead. And your mother. . . .' More silence. 'She still has the scars, Josh. The one that shows, and the deeper one, here.' He tapped the boy's chest.

'I went after them, Josh. All three of them.' He stood up, pacing the room like a caged wolf. 'I left your mother and Jake in a hospital in Socorro; buried my mother and the baby, and then I went after them.

'Two years, Josh. I followed them for two years. I got Dunbar in Kansas City. Three months later, I found Santree. He was holed up in the Guadalupes, heading for old Mexico. And then I went looking for Cantrell.'

He paused, quiet, as it all came back. 'Cantrell was from Galveston; with Galveston money; old money. He was the one who had hired the others, the one who lost out to me for the rifle. It was a game for him; nothing but a game, and the

Winchester was the prize.

'He hired men to guard him. A lot of men.' Kincaid's face was hard, the fading light from the window drawing dark lines and shadows, chiseling the fine features until there was a fierceness in him, in his eyes. 'I killed them, Josh. All of them. Five,' he said, holding up one hand, the fingers spread wide. 'And then I took Cantrell.'

J.T. was at the window now, staring outside at the distant mountains, finding no comfort in them. 'I thought it would end there, with Cantrell,' he said softly. 'But I was wrong.' He paused, rolling his shoulders as if carrying a great weight and wanting relief. 'His family hired Savage. It wasn't bounty money, Josh. Not like the law puts on you. More like . . .' He couldn't find the words.

'Savage had been in San Francisco, had competed for the Winchester. He was like the others at first; it was the rifle he wanted. And then, Cantrell's family offered him money, a lot of money.

'I was tired, Josh. I'd been on the run for two years. *Two years.* Running. Hiding. Knowing that your mother was here, and that she needed me.

'She'd taken my mother's maiden name – Kincaid – she and Jake. They came here from Socorro, to this place. . . .' He was quiet again, remembering the emptiness of those years, the loneliness. 'I came home just once in those two years, Josh. Like a thief, sneaking into my own home in the middle of the night, sneaking out just before dawn. And all the time knowing that Savage was somewhere behind me; always behind me.

'So I led him on a chase. Back to Texas; back to the old house outside of Dos Robles. And he followed me.' He turned, facing his son. 'I don't know what Savage told you; I don't want to know. But I didn't ambush him from behind. I offered to buy him off.' The man said the words as if he were ashamed; as if he was afraid his son would think him a coward for trying to buy his way out. 'I didn't have enough money;

132

nowhere near enough.

'I didn't know that Cantrell's family had upped the reward, that they had offered Savage twenty-five thousand dollars' – the thought of what $25,000 meant to a man in those years; what that money would have bought – 'twenty-five thousand dollars, and a promise that he could keep the rifle.' J.T. was quiet again; a long, morose quiet.

'Savage carried an old Navy Colt in those days, and he was good. Damned good. But I had a lot more to lose, Josh, and I'd spent a long time running; staying alive.

'He was on horseback. We weren't fifteen feet apart. I'd made my offer, and he just laughed. He said that before the day was over, he'd have my head, whatever cash I was carrying, the rifle, and twenty-five thousand waiting for him at the nearest Wells Fargo Bank.

'I was on foot, covering him with the Winchester. That's when he pulled down on me. He was mounted, and his horse bolted. That's the only thing that kept me alive; the horse jumping, and Savage's pistol hanging up in the holster. I hit the ground and fired; once, just once. Just as the horse took the bit and corkscrewed. The bullet went into the back of Savage's leg and came out through his knee. You could hear the bone shatter. . . .' J.T. inhaled, the sound cutting into the black silence. 'His horse went over, pinned Savage to the ground, and he lost his pistol.

'I'd already levered a second round into the chamber, Josh. I could have blown his head off. But I was sick of it, sick of all the killing, and sick of being alone. I wanted to come home. *I just wanted to come home.*' The words came in a hoarse whisper.

'I took Savage's pistol, tossed it into the old well. And then I left him. Not to die, Josh. Because when I got to Dos Robles, I sent a doctor back to patch him up.

'And then I came back here. Sold the horse I'd been riding, got rid of the clothes I'd worn.' He touched the

133

mustache on his upper lip. 'Grew this. The only thing I could-
n't take a chance on selling or be seen with was the rifle. So I
brought it home, Josh. Wrapped it up, tossed it in the bottom
of that trunk and forgot it all; the rifle, Jason Kilkenny.
Savage.

'For twenty years,' he finished.

Josh was on his feet. He joined his father at the window. He
reached out, fingering the handwoven cloth that covered the
small table between the beds. 'I heard Uncle Jake tell Doc
Harper to let him die, and then – at Fulton's – I saw Uncle
Jake hit him.' He was still working the thing over in his mind,
torn between his feelings for Savage and the conflict with his
uncle. 'And then, when' – he stared at his feet – 'when I was
drunk,' he said softly, 'I heard Uncle Jake say that he tried to
kill him.' He was quiet again, trying hard to find something to
justify his anger. . . 'He never said *anything*, Pa, when I found
the rifle. . . .' He was still reaching, searching for something
to excuse his behavior. *To excuse the things he had done.*

Kincaid laid his hand on the boy's shoulder. 'He was trying
to protect me, Josh. To protect me and to keep a promise
he'd made your mother, a long time ago.' J.T. saw the questions in his son's face. 'To never tell, Josh,' he said, answering
the question before the boy could ask. 'To never tell you or
Will, or anyone else.'

Josh grabbed his father's arm. '*I* told, Pa. I told Savage.
About the rifle; about Uncle Jake!'

Kincaid wrapped his arms around his son in a massive,
forgiving bear-hug. 'It doesn't matter, Josh,' he breathed, a
great weight lifted from him. 'Not anymore. Cantrell's people
are dead; all of them. And Savage. . . .' He shrugged. 'Savage
is wanted. He killed a Texas lawman in an argument over
bounty money. There'll be a federal marshal coming, Josh; to
take Savage. They'll put him away, son, for a long time.'

Josh pushed himself away from his father's chest. His
fingers were busy with the dresser scarf again, picking at it.

The cloth slipped aside, uncovering the magazine that had been stuffed beneath it. Josh's hand recoiled, his fingers feeling as though he had touched fire. Kincaid saw the move, and reached out.

He picked up the book, staring at the cover. 'Your mother said she took this away from you,' he said evenly.

Josh chewed on his bottom lip, wishing himself five years old. His ears ached, and the skin on his chest felt two sizes too small for his frame. 'I took it out of the trash, Pa.'

The book was beneath his nose. *The damned book with all the stories about Savage and Earp and Doc Holliday.*

All the lies. 'Savage isn't in jail, Pa,' he said, wishing the tears would come. 'Last night, after Ma went to sleep, I helped him, Pa.' The panic was in his chest again, in his belly. He felt an urgent need to go to the outhouse. '*I went into town and helped him break out!*'

Kincaid still held on to the book. His hand knotted into a fist, crumpling the paper; and then he relaxed, and the pages slowly unfurled. 'My God, Josh,' he breathed, not believing. Not wanting to believe. Angry, he grabbed the boy's arm. 'What the hell were you thinking, Josh?' He shook the boy, turning him loose as he saw the fear. Forcing himself, he took a deep breath, holding on to his temper. The book rattled in his hand. He held it up. 'You read this trash,' he said. 'You believed it!' He smoothed out the rumpled cover, shoving it in front of the boy's nose. 'Look at it,' he ordered. '*I said look at it!*' He tapped the brittle paper with his forefinger; the gaudy lithograph. 'Savage,' he said, pointing to the foremost figure. He moved his finger, picking out the smaller image in the rear, the drawing of a man with upraised hands. 'It's a lie, Josh,' he said, hammering at the paper with his forefinger. 'All a lie.' He saw the confusion in the boy's face; the turmoil. 'Savage never took any man prisoner, Josh,' he continued, his voice hard. 'Not once in all the years he was on the hunt. He never took a man alive!'

Josh stared at the book; at the picture on the cover. A myriad of similar pictures raced through his mind; illustrations from other dime novels. They were all the same. Two men facing each other in a dusty street, one the hero, one the outlaw; squaring off, backing away from each other, their hands poised above holstered pistols. Other scenes of men who had been shot, suspended in the air with bloodied arms.

But nobody died. They were captured; they went to jail. They fell; bit the dust, but nobody ever really died!

His father's words came to him then. Loud. Screaming to him in his mind. *He never took a man alive.*

The boy felt a deep stab of pain, still haunted by the memory of all the drawings. The suspended figures all collapsed to the ground, fell to the floor.

Died.

'I know where he is, Pa,' he said, the words coming in a low whisper, his throat burning.

J.T. was in the barn, dressed for the trail. Denim jeans, a dark-blue shirt; a leather vest stained deep brown from years of exposure to the changing elements and the man's own sweat. He looked like what he was in the beginning, what he had been before; a Texas cattleman, a working Texas cattleman. Hard. Lean. Tempered like fine steel by the fires of the time and hard work.

Only the rifle set him apart. He worked the lever once, twice, a third time; finally satisfied with the feel of the mechanism.

He still felt an affinity for the weapon. It had been a part of him, a vital part of his being. Even now, after all the years that had passed, he relished the feel of the gun in his hands.

Jake had always been the more proficient with a handgun. He had been born with an uncanny ability to use either hand equally well, and he excelled with the smaller weapon.

But not J.T. His talent lay with the long gun, the rifle. Even as a boy, he had displayed a deadly sense of machine-like accuracy. His mother had encouraged him. More than once, J.T. had provided the only meat for their table. And later, when he was almost a man, his ability with a rifle had bought their way out of Texas.

Had bought him this rifle. He hefted the piece in his hands, marveling at its balance, and then, one at a time, he began feeding the shells into the empty chamber. 'Where are the boys?'

Sarah handed her husband the oil-soaked toweling, watching as J.T. wiped the barrel a final time. 'Will is in the corral, saddling your horse.' Her face was drawn, tense, her manner subdued. 'I told Josh to stay with Carrie.' She was quiet for a moment, her eyes following the reflected beams of light that danced on the decorative ovals. 'It's true, isn't it? All the things Jake has always said. That you never lose the gift' – the word offended her – 'once you've had it.' Her cheeks colored and she was angry. 'My God, how I hate it,' she said, her hand hovering above the barrel of the Winchester. It looked like an extension of her husband's arm, a part of his physical being.

Kincaid canted the rifle across his shoulder. He pressed the back of his left hand against the woman's cheek, stroking the velvet softness of her skin. 'It's getting late, Sarah. . . .'

She nodded. 'I know.' She took his hand in both of hers, leaning into his caress. 'I'm sorry you didn't kill Savage, J.T. All those years ago, when I begged you to stop. I'm sorry you listened.' She kissed his fingertips, releasing him from a promise he made a long time ago.

They left the barn together, J.T.'s arm around the woman's waist. *Lord, she's strong*, Kincaid thought. She had always been a source of strength for him. The one good thing – besides Jake – that he had brought with him out of the Hell that was Texas.

'I want to go with you, Pa.' Will was at the corral gate. He looked young, much younger than his nineteen years.

Too young, Kincaid mused. Out loud he said, 'You'll stay here, Will, with your mother. And you'll do as she tells you. *Everything* she tells you.' He turned, shoving the Winchester into the gun boot. 'Sarah. . . .' He faced the woman again, pulling her close.

'I know what to do, J.T.,' she said. She held him, her face buried against his chest, and then lifted her head, searching for his lips. They kissed, reluctant to part, and held on to each other for a long time.

He mounted the gelding and left at a full gallop, pausing on the rim above the ranch to look back just one more time, and then he was gone.

Sarah took her son's arm, ushering him toward the house. 'I want all the stock fed before dark, Will, and the animals put in the barn. And then you're to come into the house.' Purposefully, she climbed the porch stairs, mindful of the hollow sound beneath her feet.

Silently, they went about the business of their chores. Will returned to the house. He stood at the stove, coaxing a new fire from the banked coals, watching his mother.

She was at the table, the double-barreled shotgun in her hands. There was no urgency in her, just a methodical business-as-usual certainty in the way she moved, as if loading a shotgun were as much a part of her day as setting the table or changing the baby's diaper.

'Why, Mother?' Will crossed the room.

'Because your father may not find Savage in time,' she answered. She snapped the shotgun closed. 'Get your brother, Will. We're going to have an early supper.'

Will backed away from the table, still not satisfied with his mother's answer. It seemed that there was more, something more that she was leaving unsaid. He stood for a time, shaking his head, and then headed for his parents' bedroom.

He called from the doorway, his hand still on the knob. 'Ma!'

Sarah hurried down the hallway, the shotgun resting against her right hip. She peered into the bedroom, swearing softly at what she saw.

The window was wide open, the flowered sack-cloth curtains fluttering lazily in the afternoon breeze. Carrie lay in the center of the double bed, asleep on her stomach, her legs tucked under her belly.

Josh was gone.

CHAPTER 13

The boy was on foot, running as if he were pursued by unseen demons, his arms pumping in cadence with his labored breathing. The back of his shirt was wet with sweat, and there were dark, damp circles beneath both arms. The wind touched him, chilling him, and he stumbled, going to his knees.

He scrambled back to his feet, grimacing at the pain in his scraped knees, and began to run again. His chest rose and fell, great spasms of pain tearing at his lungs, and he clenched his teeth, his eyes on the far horizon.

On the Sweet. If he could just make it to the small arroyo at the mouth of the Sweet. . . . He forced himself to move faster, oblivious to the ache in the long muscles in the back of his legs.

His mind raced, too. Savage. The name echoed in his head over and over, in time with the rise and fall of his pounding feet. *Savage . . . Savage . . . Savage. . . .*

He wished to God he had never heard the name.

Jake Kincaid paused at the fork in the road, debating which path he would take. He was tired but elated, a feeling of near peace filling him. By this time next week, Savage would be old news; a shackled prisoner being carted away by a federal lawman. *With luck,* Jake mused darkly, *straight to some Texas hangman.* He kicked his right foot free from the stirrup, looping it over the saddle horn as he lit a cigarette. His mind was made up. He was going home; back to the ranch. He was going to take the time to sit down with Josh and tell him all the things he couldn't tell him before; the things he had promised Sarah he would never tell, and it would be all right. And then he would go into town and beg Clara Altman to marry him, badge or no badge.

He stretched, lowering his leg and shoving his boot back into the stirrup. Standing upright in the saddle, he made a fist and massaged the ache in his lower back. It was growing cool; too cool for just a shirt and vest. Half-turning, he pulled his jacket from behind the saddle, easing the denim garment over his arms. He cursed, the hem of his coat catching on the pistol. *J.T. was right*, he thought. *On the trail, the Remington was as useless as tits on a boar: a real pain in the ass.*

It was different in town. He grinned. The pistol made an effective head-thumping tool for subduing an obnoxious Saturday night drunk, and occasionally it served as an impressive method for getting a man's attention when talk failed.

He reached down and unbuckled the belt, pulling the strap from around his lean waist. He wrapped the belt around the holster, and shoved it into his saddle-bags. Then he turned the gelding toward the rim trail, the one leading south along the banks of the Sweet. Towards home.

Savage tensed, the sound of loose gravel spurring him awake. He scrambled up from his resting place, hobbling stiff-legged to the mouth of the cave. Reaching out, he put his hand over the thoroughbred's nose, stifling the animal's attempted whicker, holding the beast still until the noise from below faded. The bounty hunter turned the horse loose and moved out of the cave, going to the outcroppings above the rim.

Careful not to cast a shadow, he looked down from the ledge, seeing the lone rider; noting the lean face shadowed by the dark Stetson. There was something familiar in the set of

141

the man's shoulders, and the easy way he sat his mount. Savage rubbed his eyes and looked again. He could see the dark, almost black hair thick and curly at the man's collar, and the rich cast of the man's neck against his chambray shirt. The years had been good to Kilkenny. Too good.

There was a panic in Savage, a momentary sense of betrayal. The kid had told him that Kilkenny was in Tucson; would be, for another full day. He thought, then, about the deputy, and wondered if Belmont had been found, or if the boy's mother had caught him on his return home. Caught him and somehow wormed or whipped the truth from him. She could have done it; she was strong enough, formidable enough.

The bounty man was sweating, great beads of perspiration forming at his neck, behind his ears. He shook off the tension. The kid wouldn't have told; he was sure of that. And the deputy. . . . He grinned, remembering the sound that had come when he had kicked the man's face. No. Belmont wouldn't be in any shape to say anything. Not for a while. Not until the doc had a chance to patch up the broken bones in the man's face and nose.

It was luck, he decided. An omen. After twenty years of dry runs, Lady Luck had finally chosen to smile on him. He fingered the LeMat and hurried across the top of the small escarpment. He remembered the trail, the narrow path down the side of the canyon that the boy had told him about; the hidden pathway that led down to the arroyo floor. He was sweating again, this time from the effort he was forced to expend when pushing himself beyond a walk. He swung the rigid left leg from the hip, like a pivot, balancing on the stiff leg as he threw himself forward in an awkward, time-consuming run, slipping and sliding down the steep grade.

He reached the bottom of the small canyon ahead of Kilkenny. He could hear the man's horse behind him, around the small bend at his back. He picked out the protection of a wind-eroded cluster of tall sandstone spires, wedging himself into the shadows. Pressing his back into the warm stone, he held his breath and waited.

The man on horseback moved at a slow trot, almost asleep in the saddle, his head bobbing against his chest. Savage studied the man again, his chest swelling. It was Kilkenny! The kid had been right! He waited until the horse passed his hiding place and then stepped out, drawing the LeMat. 'Kilkenny!'

Jake bolted upright in the saddle, pulling the bay up short, the single word erasing the years and taking him back to a time and place far away. He struggled to keep his seat when the horse reared up, both hands on the saddle horn when the animal landed hard on its stiff forelegs. Slowly, he turned the horse, facing the direction from which the voice had come. He kept his hands well away from his naked hips. 'Savage,' he breathed, his voice hoarse from lack of sleep.

'Been a long time, Jason.' Savage stepped out from the rocks, looking as formidable and as enduring as the landscape at his back.

The lawman held his tongue, his hat still pulled low on his forehead. He nodded at the man, seeing the gun. 'Not long enough, Rance,' he said finally.

'This makes it easier, Kilkenny,' Savage said. He was laughing. 'I was worried about how I'd handle the kid while I took my pound of flesh.' He shook his head. 'Helpful little bastard,' he said amicably. 'Busted me right out of your jail. Told me all about you; about the rifle. The whipping.' He shook a finger at the man, mocking him. 'You shouldn't have paddled the kid, Jason. Made him bitter; downright bitter.'

Jake allowed the horse to dance under him, the animal mincing away, bit by bit. 'He's young, Savage. He'll learn it was for his own good, and then he won't be bitter anymore.'

The bounty hunter laughed again. 'I don't think so.' He raised his eyebrows, enjoying the game, and amused by the idea that had just crossed his mind. 'Hell. He's going to bring me the rifle, Jason! And then I'm going to take him with me; teach him a trade. *My* trade!' The man's lips parted in a wide grin as he contemplated the irony of the thing. 'Yep!' he repeated. 'Going to teach the little bastard all I know.'

Jake tensed, his head coming up slightly, his jaws tight. 'Like hell you are, Savage!' he roared. He kicked the bay into a run, bearing down on the man.

Savage lifted the LeMat, his arm straight out as he switched the hammer to the shot position and cocked the piece. He held his fire, coldly standing his ground as the horse scrambled toward him, the animal's shod hoofs slipping against the loose gravel. He waited until the horse was almost on him, and then he fired.

The gelding folded up on his knees, the white blaze on its face freckled with its own blood, a ragged, fist-sized hole between the dead eyes. Jake was thrown up and over the animal's neck. He hit the ground with a thud, his shoulder tucked, and somersaulted into the roadway. He lay there on his belly, the wind knocked out of him, stunned.

Savage hobbled over to where the man lay. 'I've been waiting a long time for this, Kilkenny,' he said to the man's back. 'A long time.' Adjusting the hammer a second time, he cocked the piece and fired. One shot, directly into the back of the downed man's left leg.

Jake's scream mingled with the screech of a startled hawk. He convulsed, recoiling with the impact of the shot. Then, stubbornly, he pulled himself up on his good knee. The ground beneath him was wet with blood, his hands slipping as he struggled to crawl towards his downed horse. Savage was like a man possessed. He followed beside the lawman, watching as the man tried to crawl.

Jake fought the blackness that threatened to take him, struggling to right himself. He had the terrifying sensation that he was dragging something dead behind him; something dead and heavy. The pain tore at him in waves, shooting up his crotch toward his belly, subsiding, then coming again. He half-turned, clawing at the front of his coat, and heard Savage cock the piece again.

`No-o-o-oo-o!'

Savage heard the scream as it resounded the length of the canyon and echoed above the creek. He turned and saw the image of the boy silhouetted against the rise. The kid was on foot, running, stumbling pell-mell across the rugged terrain.

The bounty man heard more. His quarry was clawing his way through the rocks; moving, inching away from the gunman. Savage turned back to the lawman, ignoring the boy, and saw the man try to once more push aside his coattails.

Savage fired, Jake slumping belly down into the dirt just as Savage pulled the trigger. The shot tore into the man's lower back, and the tan jacket turned bright scarlet.

Josh was down the incline, his pants torn, his hands and knees bleeding. He ran past Savage, going down on both knees as he slid to the place where his uncle lay. 'Jake. . . .' He turned the man's face to him, brushing the sand and gravel away from his eyes, his mouth.

The man coughed, blood trickling out of the corner of his mouth. He began to laugh, a sick sound bubbling up from the depths of his belly. He lifted his hand, a single finger pointing directly at Savage. 'You're going to hang, bounty man.' The laughter gave way to a wet wheeze, and then resumed. Soft; mocking. He tugged at his buttons, his fingers numb. Josh reached down, touching his uncle's cold hands. Jake nodded, giving the boy's hand a quick squeeze. He winked, grinning a lopsided grin that turned into a sudden grimace, holding his words until the boy had finished with the buttons. 'No gun, Savage,' he croaked finally. He tore open the coat, exposing his empty hips. '*No gun!*'

Savage limped over to the fallen lawman, his face contorted. He grabbed Josh away, staring down at the man's hips in disbelief. And then he lifted his eyes to the man's face.

145

He stumbled back a full pace, his mouth dropping open. *Brown. The man's eyes were brown!* Enraged – cheated – Savage cursed. Jason Kilkenny's eyes were blue; china blue, almost luminescent. Ice, the last time he'd seen them. Blue ice. 'Who the hell are you?' he shouted, grabbing the man's coat.

'The brother,' Jake breathed. 'Jason Kilkenny's brother.' The laughter came again, bringing a renewed stream of red blood to the man's mouth, and still he struggled to speak. 'You've killed an unarmed man, Savage,' he rasped, 'and as sure as there's a sun in the heavens, you're going to hang. . . .'

Savage swore, loud, raising the pistol high above the lawman's head. 'Goddamn you!' he cursed, and his own words mocked him as they echoed from the towering rocks.

'*Rance!*'

Savage turned, squinting into the setting sun. He saw the outline of the man; the stance. He swung his eyes back to the man on the ground, and then to the almost mirror image that shimmered in the light before him. 'Jason?' he roared.

'Jason,' the other answered. He stood there, his hands at his sides. 'Been a long time since Texas, Rance,' he said softly. He swung his eyes to his fallen brother and felt something deep inside him die. *My fault,* he agonized. *All my fault. . . .*

'Twenty years, Jason,' the man-hunter answered, his brown eyes burning. The LeMat was still in his hand. He stared across at his adversary. 'You should have killed me, Jason,' he intoned. He lifted the LeMat, and stepped forward.

'Pa!' Josh was on his feet. He scrabbled away from his uncle, charging at Savage's spread legs.

It was instinct that moved the bounty killer. Years of watching his back, responding spontaneously to sudden noise, sudden threat. He spun around, and fired.

A second shot echoed in his ears, simultaneous with his own. There was an intense burning between his shoulder blades, and then another explosion as he turned to face the pain. He fell to one knee, the lame leg rigid behind him, the

146

second bullet tearing into his gut just above his belt buckle. He looked up, the sun glinting off something bright, something moon white and sunshine yellow. Silver and gold.

The Winchester. Savage's eyes opened wide, greed lighting them a final time. He stretched out his arm, still reaching for the prize, and slid to the ground. His long fingers closed around a fist full of empty air.

J.T. dropped the gun, sprinting to where his son and brother lay. He knelt between them, tugging at them both and drawing them close as he sunk to the ground.

Josh opened his eyes, a fire deep in his thigh. 'Pa?' He lifted his head, his eyes settling first on Savage, and then on the pale face on his father's other knee. 'Uncle Jake...' Sobbing, he reached out, 'I'm sorry . . .' He wanted to say more, but was swallowed up by a black, starless oblivion, the stench of death all around him.

CHAPTER 14

Faces. For days the boy drifted, seeing only faces. Heads, detached from their bodies, floating above him; at his side. His mother's. Doc Harper's. Will. And Jake; pale, distant. Fading.

There was pain. Intense pain. In his left leg, tingling down its full length, like when he was small, and he'd stood next to a tree still smoldering from a charge of lightning.

Then, on the morning of the fifth day, he was lucid. Just for a short time. He looked over at the bed where his uncle had lain.

It was empty.

He slept, then. On and off, for countless more days, his skin wet and clammy with fever. The dark frightened him, the searing glow of the lamp even more, and his dreams were filled with the things he had seen and heard. Over and over he saw it; the blood, the horror.

The boy's eyelids fluttered, and he awoke. His skin felt cool, refreshingly cool; his insides empty, cavernous. His eyes probed the room, adjusting to the light as they came to rest on the sleeping giant in the dark corner. 'Pa?'

J.T. roused, lifting himself up out of the chair, his bones cracking in noisy rebellion to his efforts. He moved noiselessly to the side of the bed. 'It's been a long time, Josh,' he said gently, brushing the hair from the boy's eyes. 'A long time.' He went to the door, calling for his wife, and they came back to the boy's bed together. The woman dropped down on her knees beside the bed, her lips warm on the boy's forehead. 'Thank God,' she breathed. She held him, her tears warming his cheek.

They took turns feeding him, rationing the rich broth his mother had prepared, later helping him with small glasses of cool, fresh milk. He still felt empty inside, even after his mother said he'd had enough. 'You'll get sick, Josh,' she smiled.

Then she left, and the boy was alone with his father. He stared across at the empty bed. 'Uncle Jake?' he asked quietly, hoping that some of his dreams were just that; bad dreams that faded with the daylight.

J.T. reached out, his hand hovering at the boy's forehead. There was no easy way to excuse death – he had learned that as a child, and the lessons had continued long into his manhood. 'He's dead, Josh,' he answered. He held the boy, rocking him like an infant until the tears stopped, and the boy slept again.

Doc Harper was at the kitchen table. He reached down, snapping his bag shut, avoiding Kincaid's eyes. 'You look like hell, J.T.,' he observed. 'You and Sarah both.'

Kincaid nodded, his gaze on the cup of coffee that was growing cold in his hands. 'It's been six weeks, Doc.' He downed the coffee, hoping to ease the fire that constantly burned in his belly.

Harper was still fumbling with the straps on his satchel. 'You've got to get him out of that room, J.T.; out of this house.' He rolled his shoulders, easing the cramp in his neck, hoping to shake off the black cloud that had descended on him when he entered the home. 'All of you. You need to get on with the business of living.' He held up his hand, silencing the other.

'Josh isn't a cripple, J.T.' He tapped his head. 'In here, he thinks he's a cripple; that God's punishing him, making him pay for what happened to Jake.' He hesitated, and then resumed speaking, his eyes on the man. 'You've got to get him on his feet more, make him use that leg. Soon, J.T. Real soon.'

Kincaid reached out, fingering the man's black bag. 'Have anything in there for grief, Doc? For guilt?' There was bitter sarcasm in the man's words.

'No,' the doctor answered. 'And even less for self pity.' He raked the man with his eyes. 'Jake is dead. Nothing can change that.' The physician was quiet a moment; reflective. 'It's Josh's sickness,' he said softly, his hand going to the man's shoulder. 'But it's spreading. To you, to Sarah. Even Will and Carrie. You can stop it, J.T.' He tightened his grip on the man. 'Or you can let it go on until it makes Josh the same thing that Savage was.' He let his hand slip from Kincaid's shoulder. 'Boseman's going to be in Sonoita, J.T. Word is, he's bringing some prize stock through, on his way into Mexico.'

Kincaid nodded, half-hearing the man's words. 'Next week, Doc. Will you come next week?'

Harper inhaled. 'I'll come,' he agreed. 'I don't know what the hell good it will do, but I'll come.' He picked up his bag and went out the door, pausing to hold the screen open for the woman.

Kincaid watched as his wife came into the kitchen, saw the way she jumped when the door slammed shut at her back. He reached out, taking the basket of clothes that she carried. His eyes swept her face, and he swallowed at what he saw. The joy was gone from her eyes, the fire. He lifted his gaze to the mirror on the wall and studied his own reflection, and saw the same gaunt emptiness marked him as well. He pulled Sarah close, trying to remember the last time he had bedded her; that he had been able to bed her. 'We have to talk, Sarah,' he said softly, burying his head n the comfort of her hair. 'About Josh,' he breathed. 'About what we're doing to him.'

*

Josh was awake. He had dressed, and was thumping around the room leaning heavily on the crutch Will had fashioned for him. He was impatient, hungry; aware of the sounds and smells of breakfast. Anxious, he hobbled over to the table beside the bed, reaching for the bell that his mother had placed there the first morning he had wakened, the morning he had finally come back to the world of the living. He rooted around the pile of litter on the table, his movement frantic. It was gone. The bell was gone! He cursed, thumping his way across the room to the doorway, his left leg stiff. 'Ma!' He waited, and then called out again, louder. '*Ma!*'

There was a silence, and then the soft murmur of hushed conversation. He heard the slow scrape of a chair, followed by the sound of footsteps coming down the narrow hallway. Heavy, booted feet. He limped back to the bed, expectant.

Will appeared in the doorway. He inhaled, feeling awkward, and delivered his message. 'Pa says you're to come to the table, Josh.'

Josh sat on the edge of the bed, his mouth agape. He stared at the doorway long after his brother had disappeared. Then he swore, vehemently, the anger coloring his face. His stomach began to rumble, and there was a hungry gnawing deep down in his gut. The smells from the kitchen became even more enticing.

Kincaid was at the table, his hands busy with a piece of freshly baked bread and a butter knife. He looked up, watching as the boy worked his way down the hallway, the angry thump-bump of the crutch echoing across the plank flooring. 'Josh,' he greeted. He gestured at the empty place on his left. 'Sit down.'

The boy did as he was told, his eyes on his plate, his elbows on the table. He sat there, waiting. Kincaid reached out, cupping the boy's chin in his palm. 'Something wrong with your arms, too, Josh?' he asked, the words scathing, sarcastic.

The boy stared up at him, his lips a tight line. He shook his head and pulled away from his father's touch. Silently, he reached out, filling his plate, wondering why his mother had not intervened or offered to help.

'Are we still going into town, Pa?' Will was concentrating on his plate, sawing at a piece of thick side meat.

'I don't know why not,' the elder Kincaid answered. 'I hear that Bosman's got a two-year-old colt with him; King Ranch stock. I thought I'd take a look at him, see if he's everything Boseman claims him to be.'

Will nodded, stuffing the piece of meat into his mouth. 'For stud, Pa?' The youth chewed his meat thoughtfully, remembering the first time he had seen a King Ranch stallion.

J.T. shrugged. 'Could be,' he said. He turned his eyes on his youngest son. 'That sorrel mare of yours, Josh. Bred right, she ought to throw a good foal.'

Josh's head came up. 'She's mine!' He had trained the mare from a yearling for working cattle. 'She's riding stock,' he argued. 'Riding stock!'

Kincaid leaned back in his chair, his eyes meeting briefly with his wife's. 'Since when?' He reached out, fingering the boy's crutch. 'This is a working ranch, Josh. That means an animal earns its keep, or . . .' He didn't finish. He stood up, drinking the last of his coffee. 'Will,' he called.

The young man wiped his chin and excused himself. 'I'll get the horses saddled, Pa.' He headed for the door, hesitating as his father held him back. The man held up three fingers, nodding his head at Josh. Will grinned and went out the door.

Kincaid picked up his plate and carried it to the sink. He turned, facing his youngest son. 'You're going to town with us, Josh,' he said.

The boy sat hunched over his plate. He shook his head. 'No,' he said finally. He began rubbing at the stiffness in his left leg, his fingers working the flesh above his tender knee.

Kincaid inhaled, his eyes on the top of the boy's bent head. 'That wasn't an invitation, Josh. I'm telling you that you're going.' He wiped his face, dusting the bread crumbs from his mustache. 'Let's go.'

Josh's hands knotted into fists, one on either side of his plate. He swallowed, his lower lip jutting out stubbornly. He refused to look at the man, watching as his father's big hands took away his still full plate, his knife and fork.

Sarah Kincaid sat at the table, still feeding the baby. She reached out, touching the boy's arm. 'You do as your father tells you, Joshua.'

The boy felt as if he was being attacked from all sides. 'I can't, Ma,' he whispered, pleading with her.

The woman lifted the baby from the highchair, balancing her on one hip. 'You won't know until you try, will you?' She turned, carrying the child back down the hallway, determined not to give in. She could feel the boy's eyes on her back. *Birthing them, allowing them to grow up, finally letting them go . . . the pain was just as intense no matter if it was the beginning or the end.* She hugged her daughter closer, taking solace in the baby's laugh, and closed the bedroom door behind her.

'Josh!' Kincaid summoned his youngest son, calling him from the porch.

The boy rose up from his chair, grabbing the crutch. Angry, he thumped across the kitchen floor, balancing on his good leg as he jabbed the screen door open with a vicious poke from his stick. He hobbled across the porch to the place where his father stood waiting; hating the sound of the crutch, hating his sire even more. Stiffly, he negotiated the narrow stairs, following after his father, and felt the sudden rush of sweat to his forehead and neck.

Kincaid started toward the barn. He could hear the boy limping along behind him, the dull tattoo of the crutch plopping against the dry, packed ground. He stopped, shaking his head when he saw Will leading the horses from the barn, signaling for him to stay at the corrals. Turning, he looked at his youngest son, his eyes sweeping the boy with a fleeting glance of pity. He reached out, testing the padding at the top of the crutch with this thumb and forefinger. He cocked his head. 'You move like that thing hurts your arm,' he said, solicitous. 'Let me have a look. . . .'

Josh hesitated, leaning heavily on the crutch. His eyes were on the narrow, rock-covered cairn in the field beyond the house. Jake's grave. His throat began to burn, and he turned, pivoting, heading back toward the house.

'Joshua!' Kincaid called to his son again. He held out his hand, pointing to the crutch, and waggled a finger at the boy.

Reluctantly, Josh responded to the man's offer of help. He balanced on his good leg, swinging the crutch out from beneath his left armpit.

Kincaid took the stick, avoiding the boy's eyes as he felt himself weakening. He hefted the crutch in his palm, as if testing it for balance, and then let it slip through his fingers. He caught it by the bottom tip, his hand closing around the blunted nub. Then, swinging it in a wide circle, he let go, heaving the thing high into the air. He watched as it cartwheeled, hearing the sound as it sliced through the air; the stick turning end over end as it spun away from them. It thudded against the side of the barn, splitting, the two disjointed pieces falling into a high mound of straw and manure.

'No!' Josh stared up at the man. He stood there on one leg, hopping as he tried to maintain his equilibrium. He looked over his shoulder to the house, seeing his mother in the doorway, his eyes smarting as she retreated from view and shut the thick inner door. And then he swung his gaze to his father.

Kincaid was walking toward the barn again, moving away from the boy with lengthening strides. Grim-faced, he shook his head at his eldest son a second time, holding up his hand when the boy started towards him with the three mounts.

154

He pulled himself into the saddle, his hands folded across the saddle horn as he stared down at his youngest son. Josh stood there, his face drained of color. He was in the middle of the yard, teetering on the good leg, an equal distance from the house and the corral.

The boy faced his father fully. His right leg was getting tired. He crow-hopped again, twice, trying to steady himself, remaining in the same spot. 'Damn you,' he breathed. The words swelled in his throat, building with the pain in his weary right knee. '*Goddamn you!*' This time he shouted the words, shaking his fist at the man.

Kincaid remained unmoved. He took his gloves out of his pockets, easing them in place. Reaching down with his right hand, he unfastened his rope. 'You're going to use that leg, Josh,' he said. 'How you use it is up to you.' He shook out a loop.

'Pa!' Will reached up to the man, his face white. His eyes darted to his brother, and then back to his father. 'Let me help him, Pa. . . .'

'Get mounted, Will,' Kincaid ordered softly, his gaze never leaving his youngest son. 'Now. And then you stay here, right here, or so help me God, I'll use this rope on you.' He cut his eyes at the boy, his lips a tight line.

'Yes, sir,' Will murmured, yielding to the man's gaze. Silently, he climbed aboard his horse, his eyes on the ground, unable to watch.

Josh was still in the center of the large yard. He watched open-mouthed as his father began spinning the rope. The man made the toss, the boy instinctively raising his arms as he ducked and spun away from the *reata*. He went down hard, rolling away from the loop, and felt the bristling scratch as the hemp brushed his cheek.

Kincaid grinned coldly, reeling in the line. 'Get up, Josh!' he ordered. He recoiled the rope quickly, building the loop again. 'Get on your feet, and walk over here like a man' – he

155

spurred the boy with his eyes – 'or I'll drag you.' The promise came through clenched teeth, the man's voice whisper-quiet.

Josh wiped a hand across his eyes. He swallowed, watching as his father began to spin the rope a second time. He scrabbled away on his hands and knees, cursing the awkward dead weight of his stiff leg. The coarse rope snaked over his shoulders and was jerked tight.

Instinctively, Kincaid's gelding backed up, the rope taut against its neck as the man pulled up the slack. The boy was jerked forward, on to his belly. He reached out with both hands, fighting the line, cursing as his father's horse continued to back up. 'Goddamn you,' he raged.

Kincaid gave the rope a sudden, fierce yank, his abrupt movement a harsh rebuke for the boy's cursing. He urged the gelding back, slowly, his eyes on the boy's face. 'You remind me of Savage,' he began, tormenting the boy with his words. 'Wallowing in self-pity; feeling sorry for yourself.' He used his spurs, still backing the horse, still pulling the rope tighter. 'Expecting everyone else to feel sorry for you!' He shook his head, hurling the final insult as he pulled the rope even tighter. 'No guts, Josh!' he roared. 'You and Savage. *No guts!*'

Furious, Josh bucked against the rope, purposely flipping himself over, his feet pointed at the horse. He dug into the dirt with his good leg, his heel scarring the ground as he fought the noose. He pulled himself forward, winding the rope around his bare hands, bracing himself as he fought for the coiled slack his father held.

The man felt the boy's sudden tug, felt the rope slide through his gloved fingers. He stopped the horse, playing a man's game of tug-of-war with the boy, bedeviling him. He gave the boy slack, pulled the rope taut again; then gave more slack. Not much, just enough to keep him fighting. He watched as the boy clawed harder and harder at the stiff line.

Hand over hand, his eyes on his father's face, Josh pulled at the lariat. Slowly, laboriously, he pulled himself upright on his good leg. He balanced there, trying to shake loose of the line, his face coloring as the man spurred the gelding backwards still another time. He felt the rope tightening, tugging at him. 'No, Pa!' He wavered on the good leg, breathing hard. The cords in his neck stood out as he felt the rope begin a slow burn through his bare hands. 'Please, Pa.'

Kincaid stopped the horse. 'You're going to come to me, Josh,' he declared. 'On your belly, or on your feet.'

The boy stood there, his shoulders heaving. He tried to wet his lips, his mouth full of dust, his throat dry. Carefully he explored his father's face, reading the look behind the unrelenting blue eyes. He nodded his head. 'On my feet, Pa,' he uttered hoarsely. 'On my feet!' Grimacing, he put his weight on his injured left leg, fighting the wave of sickness that surged through his stomach. The muscles and tendons rebelled, liquid fire coursing up and down the length of his calf and thigh. Reaching out, he grabbed the rope, and felt it go taut.

'One step at a time, son,' Kincaid urged gently.

Josh nodded again, his jaws tight. Using the rope, he pulled himself forward, his eyes matching his father's. Cold; stubborn. He paused midway, standing upright on both legs, feet spread, clenching his teeth against the pain as he used both hands to pull the hondo loose and lift the rope from his shoulders. He threw the lariat to the ground, his eyes still on his father's face, willing his lame leg to respond. Slowly, one foot in front of the other. One torturous step at a time.

He reached his father's side, burying his head against the man's leg as he composed himself. Then he pushed himself away from the gelding, lifting his eyes to meet his father's scrutiny. 'I'm here, Pa.' He took a deep breath, a prideful arrogance in him. 'On my feet,' he said. 'On my own two feet!'

Kincaid reached down, his thumb wiping away the single tear that streaked the boy's dust-caked cheek. 'About time,

Son,' he admonished, his voice soft. He lifted his head. 'Will!' he called. 'Bring the sorrel over here. We're going to town!'

Josh pushed himself away from his father's horse, shaking his head. 'No!' He turned, his eyes measuring the distance between himself and the mare. 'You stay there, Will; right there!' he ordered. Stubbornly, his head high, he limped across the yard.

Kincaid watched as Josh marched toward the mare. He remembered the boy as a babe, recalling the warm, expansive joy he had felt inside his chest when he saw the child take his first unsteady steps by himself. The feeling he was experiencing now was just the same.

He reconsidered, watching as the boy strode stubbornly across the yard, the limp less pronounced than before. *No*, he reasoned, *this was better; so much better than a baby's first shaky steps into childhood.*

This was a boy, taking the first long steps toward becoming a man.